Spring Fever

by

KERRY ALLYNE

Harlequin Books

TORONTO • NEW YORK • LOS ANGELES • LONDON
AMSTERDAM • PARIS • SYDNEY • HAMBURG
STOCKHOLM • ATHENS • TOKYO • MILAN

Original hardcover edition published in 1982
by Mills & Boon Limited

ISBN 0-373-02527-0

Harlequin Romance first edition February 1983

Never had she felt such raw emotion

Words failed her as her gaze clung helplessly to his. Groaning with desire, Corey effortlessly swung her into his arms, and as he carried her across to the bed, protest was the furthest thing from her mind. She loved him with every part of her being.

Even if her actions did allow him to guess how irrevocably her feelings were involved, it just wasn't possible to conceal them anymore.

Savoring the feel of his muscular length pressing against her, Dale recalled another time when she'd shared Corey's bed with him and had been as tantalizingly aware of his firm lips moving over the scented skin of her throat. Only on this occasion she wasn't anxious to escape....

CHAPTER ONE

IN the mid-morning quiet Dale Freeman had no difficulty at all in hearing her uncles' approach as they descended the hotel stairs, and her shapely mouth curved fondly at the sound of their wrangling voices. During the three months she had lived with them at their hotel in Queensland's Gulf country she had come to realise that these minor squabbles were part of her bachelor uncles' way of life, but were not to be taken too seriously all the same. On this occasion, and not for the first time, the intended colour for the building's exterior was the cause of their dissension.

'I can't see what's wrong with leaving it the colour it is,' stated Lester in somewhat testy tones. At seventy-one he was the elder by two years and usually thought that should automatically give him a greater say in their affairs.

His brother, Irwin, gave a disparaging snort. 'Because it's been grey for the last ten years now, that's why! It's time we had a change and did the place up a bit, especially now Dale's living with us. Girls her age like bright colours.'

'But not that hideous pink you bought because it was on special offer,' interposed Lester rapidly, derogatorily. 'We'd be the laughing stock of the town if we used that. Besides, I don't like pink. Never did,' he added as if that settled the matter.

'Well, I think it's a nice colour,' Irwin defended his

5

choice on a piqued note. 'And since we've already got the paint . . .'

'We are not painting it pink!' Lester vetoed flatly.

'We're not using grey again either!' his brother retorted immediately. He uttered a low, sly chuckle. 'That's the trouble with you fellers when you get to your age—you get too set in your ways.'

Spoken from the advantage of a mere sixty-nine years, noted Dale with no little amusement, and propping her elbows on the bar where she had just finished serving their first three customers of the day, she rested her chin on her raised and linked hands as her thoughts wandered absently to her first meeting with Lester and Irwin Freeman just a few months before.

Of course she had always known her father had two older brothers who, after returning from service in the last world war, had left Tasmania for mainland Australia in order to seek a new life for themselves. But when they had eventually bought the Club Hotel in Karraparinka some thirty years previously, the great distance separating them from their brother had naturally meant that their family contact had been reduced to the written kind. And that more and more rarely as time went by, since not one of the three was an overly-enthusiastic correspondent.

Consequently, Dale had reached her present age of twenty-two without ever having met her uncles in person. That was, except for at her christening as a baby, which had apparently been considered of sufficient importance to lure them back from the sun-baked plains in the vastness of the north to the cool, rain-washed hills of the south for a short time, because on reaching their forties her parents had just about despaired of ever having a child at all. Though, of course, Dale had no recollection of the occasion. Her only knowledge of the remaining members of her father's family had been, more or less, an address and a couple of old black and white photographs taken many years before.

Then five months ago had come the shock and disbelief of losing both her parents in a car crash and, out of courtesy, she had written to advise her uncles of the tragedy. However, her surprise at finding their sun-weathered figures on her doorstep some three weeks later had been nothing compared to the amazement she experienced when they immediately proposed she make her home with them in future.

It hadn't been a possibility she had even remotely considered—after all, her friends, her work, everything she had grown up with, were in Hobart—but as the days passed and she recovered from her initial surprise, the more receptive she had found herself becoming to their persuasions. A change of scene would probably help dispel the painful memories which kept occurring, and it would be nice to have some family members close at hand too. Also, it would give her a chance to sample a completely different way of life and, as had been pointed out, if it didn't suit her then she could always return to Tasmania at a later date.

Now, with a contented sigh, Dale reached out a hand to the wall behind her, located the switch she was feeling for, and turned the ceiling fan control up another notch before resuming her pensive pose. Even though she hadn't once regretted her decision to join her uncles in Karraparinka, she still wasn't quite acclimatised to the northern temperatures yet and, as a result, usually had the fans turning at full speed by the end of the day—a circumstance which often brought forth a good deal of amiable teasing from the locals.

At first Lester and Irwin hadn't wanted her to work in the hotel at all, but when it became obvious she had no intention of remaining idle and that, owing to the town's size—or lack thereof—there was no other work available for her, they finally had no choice but to relent and allow her to help. With no specific duties outlined, this meant that she could lend a hand wherever it was needed, and nothing gave her more pleasure than knowing she was relieving her uncles of some of their workload. At their ages she felt they should be starting to take things a little easier, and in order to accomplish this, for the last month or so she had taken it upon herself to open the bar every day so that they might at least have their mornings free.

'I hate to interrupt your daydreams, of course, but I take it you do work here, and that you're not just an extremely attractive form of decoration?'

The mockingly accented enquiry suddenly penetrated Dale's reverie, causing her to start, and bringing a self-conscious flush to her cheeks as her thickly lashed violet gaze came to rest on the tall male figure confronting her.

'I—I'm sorry,' she stammered awkwardly. 'Did you want a drink?' half turning towards the glass-fronted fridges behind her.

'No, a room, actually,' he drawled.

The faintly humorous cast of his well-shaped mouth had Dale experiencing an unaccountable surge of annoyance. 'For how long?' she countered discouragingly.

'A week, maybe two.' He shrugged broad, sloping shoulders offhandedly.

'I'm sorry, but I don't . . .'

''Struth! Corey Tavener! Fancy seeing you back in

town!' exclaimed one of the men at the other end of
the bar, and cutting Dale off in mid-sentence. With a
broad grin he began pacing towards the newcomer, a
hand reaching out before him. 'How've you been
doing, mate?'

'Not too bad, thanks, Ferris.' A responding smile
creased the slightly younger man's face as their hands
met in a firm grip. 'And you?'

'Oh, much the same as always. You know how it is,'
Ferris replied with a laugh. Then, looking over his
shoulder to his two companions who were, even then,
preparing to join him, 'Hey . . . Noel, Wally! You remember Corey, don't you?'

From their ready answers it was apparent they did,
and as they too exchanged greetings and enquiries with
the new arrival, Dale took the opportunity to study the
object of their attention unopposed.

Dark and dangerous, were the first two thoughts
that slipped into her mind as her glance travelled the
muscular length of his denim shirt and jeans-covered
frame. Her own hair was dark, but nowhere near as
black as the rather short-cropped thatch which lay
close to his self-assuredly held head, she noted. In
contrast his eyes were a warm honey brown, the irises
flecked with gold, and bordered by thick, overlong
lashes which seemed almost out of place when
compared to the rest of his bronzed and well-chiselled
features.

All in all, he gave the impression of being tough and
durable, a man's man, and yet at the same time, she
had to admit, he exuded a kind of knockabout charm
which would attract women like ants to sugar and
which she also instinctively knew could spell disaster
for the unprepared.

But ... Tavener? her thoughts rolled on curiously. Corey Tavener. That was what Ferris had called him. A relative of Black Jack Tavener out at Tavener's Bridge station, perhaps? she wondered. Their colouring was certainly similar enough for there to be some such association. He could be a nephew, she pondered thoughtfully. His age, which she judged to be about thirty-two or three, tended to suggest he might be, and as he was obviously known in town—even if she hadn't ever heard his name mentioned before—then she supposed that was most likely to be the case. After all, Tavener wasn't that common a name for there to be two completely unrelated families with the same surname in a town the size of Karra.

However, no sooner had she convinced herself of such a likelihood than another puzzled crease began to mar the smooth lines of her forehead. If he *was* family, then why was he booking into the hotel and not staying out at the Tavener homestead, and if he was known as widely in the district as he appeared to be, why hadn't Kurt ever spoken of him?

Kurt Agnew, whom Dale had been casually dating for the last two months, was Black Jack's eldest stepson, so to her way of thinking if anyone should have known about Corey Tavener then he should! Of course, having nothing more than a name to go on made it extremely difficult to fit all the pieces together, she conceded wryly, then discovered herself to be listening to the men's conversation with an interest that surprised her in an attempt to find out more about the man who was greeted so warmly, and yet whose name had never been mentioned.

Unfortunately for Dale, though, her uncles chose that moment to enter the bar, and their reaction to

Corey Tavener's presence was exactly the same as the others' had been, so that by the time their words of welcome, etcetera, had been offered, she was still no wiser than she had been before and her curiosity was rapidly being displaced by a somewhat nettled impatience. When all was said and done, she had been speaking to him first—even if a little unhelpfully—and since he had seen fit to mockingly claim her attention then he might at least have had the decency not to forgo it quite so promptly! Not if he wanted a room at all, that was, she amended quickly.

'You've heard about your father, then?' Irwin's gruff-sounding query had Dale immediately pricking her ears again.

The newcomer nodded shortly. 'Mmm, from a drover on his way south about a week ago. He said he thought he was in pretty bad shape when he left.'

'Yeah, well, I guess he was for a while, but you know Black Jack . . . he's a hard man to keep down,' inserted Ferris with a rueful half laugh.

'He's a hard man . . . period,' added Lester explicitly.

Dale, meanwhile, couldn't keep her eyes from widening in astonishment. Corey Tavener was Black Jack's *son*? That was one possibility which just hadn't occurred to her! Why would it, when Kurt, and everyone else it seemed, had kept so quiet on the subject? But it was also obvious it was Jack Tavener's recent heart attack that had brought him back to town.

Corey acknowledged Lester's remark with a wry smile and a brief hunching of one shoulder. 'But he's as tough on himself as he is on everyone else.'

'That's true,' Irwin conceded. For all of them by the looks on their faces, Dale guessed. 'There was only ever one person Jack Tavener took a soft line with, and . . .' Breaking off, much to his niece's disappointment at least, he gave a shake of his grizzled head and sighed. 'But that's another story. At the moment I'd say you'd be more interested in a drink than a discussion, wouldn't you, son?'

'You could be right, although I was in the process of trying to book in when . . .'

'And I was in middle of telling him that it might not be possible for us to put him up for two weeks,' interrupted Dale in an unusually defiant tone, but pleased to at least be able to say something!

'Why on earth not?' frowned Lester, looking at her in surprise. 'Of course we can. For as long as he wants.'

Encountering one slyly raised brow across the bar counter, Dale felt the heat of a flush climbing to her hairline. 'But we're fully booked out for the weekend after next. The races are on then, remember?' she prompted embarrassedly.

The Karraparinka Races were *the* social highlight of the year, with the town's population of a few hundred or so swelling to a couple of thousand, and with most of the visitors having to live under canvas for the two days because it just wasn't possible for the town's three hotels to accommodate them all.

'Oh, yes, I'd forgotten for the minute,' her uncle admitted vaguely. 'Not that it matters, anyway, because we can always find room somewhere for Corey. Can't we, Irwin?' He turned to his brother for corroboration.

'Yes, of course,' nodded Irwin agreeably, and unconsciously caused Dale to sigh with dissatisfaction. For some unknown reason, she felt a little discomfited at the idea of Corey Tavener staying in the hotel, and if there was one time when she wouldn't have minded her uncles having a dispute, this was it, but on this occasion it appeared they were in complete accord.

'But where?' she now had to ask, even if it did make her look unco-operative.

Lester glanced at her curiously. 'Oh, in—in . . .' he faltered.

'In the spare room next to yours,' Irwin filled in triumphantly. 'It's vacant, and although it's in our quarters, I'm sure Corey wouldn't mind.'

He might not, but Dale certainly did! 'It's such a small room, though,' she protested in simulated regret.

'That's okay, I don't plan to be spending much time in it,' Corey drawled lazily. 'As long as it's somewhere to kip down, it'll do me.' Pausing, he sent her uncles a quizzical glance. 'Since when have you two old re-probates been sharing your quarters with the staff, anyway?'

Irwin uttered a dry chuckle, his brown eyes twinkling. 'Oh, Dale's not really staff. She's our niece,' he explained proudly. 'You remember us telling you about our brother Wesley who lived in Hobart, don't you? Well, Dale's his daughter.'

'Good lord! The christening you went to all those years ago when I was a kid,' Corey suddenly laughed. 'I always remembered it because everyone kept saying how it was the only time since the day you'd arrived in Karra that you left the place.' His smiling gaze swung round to rest fully on Dale and her senses reeled crazily in response. Did he have to be quite so damned handsome! she cursed helplessly. 'Well, well . . . it's a pleasure to meet one of Les and Irwin's relatives at last. How are you, Dale?'

'Fine, thank you,' she answered in a constricted voice. At least she had been until he came on the scene!

'And how long are you intending to stay in Karraparinka?'

Before she could reply, Ferris had broken in humorously, 'All the young fellers hope it's for good. Not that most of 'em will get a look in, anyway. Kurt's already seen to that.'

'Oh?' Corey's brows lifted smoothly in unison. 'Kurt Agnew, you mean?'

'Mmm, that's who he means. These days Kurt seems to be in town more often than he's on the property,' advised Lester, and not altogether jovially. The same as he and Irwin sometimes weren't when they teased her about Kurt's interest in her, Dale recalled contemplatively.

'So who's running Tavener's Bridge while the old man's sick?' Corey immediately wanted to know. 'Karl and Louise?' From his tone it didn't sound as if he believed his stepmother and youngest stepbrother would be very successful at doing so.

'Not if Black Jack can help it, I'll be bound,' laughed Ferris. 'It'll take more than a heart attack to make him relinquish control ... to anyone.'

Corey's lips twisted obliquely. 'Whether he intended to or not, it sounds as if he already has if Kurt isn't pulling his weight.'

'Kurt does pull his weight,' Dale promptly contradicted, loyalty not allowing her to remain silent. 'He's always telling me how much work he gets through.'

Momentarily, while the others smiled and laughed— much to her irritation—at what they considered to be her biased defence. Corey's expression tightened markedly, and in that instant Dale could see a definite resemblance to his father. There was a strength in his jawline that hinted at the same ruthless streak his parent possessed. Then the image was gone as he too smiled.

'And what about the work he should be doing while he's in here telling you what he has done, hmm?' he taunted. 'I would have thought now, while they're a man down, would've been the time for him to be doing more, not less.'

'He's still entitled to *some* time off,' she persisted, although not quite so strongly. She had sometimes wondered herself if Kurt wasn't using his stepfather's illness as an excuse to take things a little easier than would otherwise have been possible. 'Or don't you think he should come in to town at all?' Her eyes held his defiantly.

'With you around, I doubt it would be possible to keep him out,' he predicted in a mockingly amused drawl. 'However, I can't see the old man being quite so understanding. There'll be hell to pay if he discovers things left undone just because there's a pretty new face in town.'

He made it sound as if she was to blame, seethed Dale indignantly, and fixed him with a resentful glare. 'Well, whatever the reason, I don't know what gives you the right to criticise,' she retorted with unfamiliar truculence. 'At least Kurt does still work on the property. You, apparently, though so much of it that you left!'

In the split second of utter silence that followed it would have been possible to hear the proverbial pin drop, and Dale promptly knew she had recklessly allowed herself to be goaded into inadvertently touching on matters there was more to than met the eye.

Nor did her uncle Lester's ensuing half embarrassed, half remonstrating, 'Dale!' help to calm her racing pulse as she waited tensely for Corey's reaction. A response which, when it came, was delivered with a deceptively soft but nonetheless acid sting.

'And you, my sweet, would do well to restrict your comments to those subjects you know something about!'

Dale dropped her amethyst gaze to the bar counter selfconsciously. 'I'm sorry,' she apologised, but more for her uncles' sakes than her own even so. Maybe she shouldn't have said what she did, but if he hadn't been so free with his remarks concerning Kurt, she probably wouldn't have!

'Yes, well, I figure it's about time we had that drink Irwin mentioned,' said Lester in a rush. 'We'll take a few cans out on to the verandah, shall we?' A suggestion which, not unnaturally, was accepted with alacrity by all those present.

'I'll pass them across to you,' offered Dale quietly, already moving towards the fridges.

'Thanks, love,' her uncle smiled back gratefully, encouragingly. 'Oh, and you'd better let us have some coolpacks too,' indicating the polystyrene containers in which the cans were usually served in order to keep them cold.

Having done as he asked, and as the men began drifting outside, Dale gave the counter a cursory wipe with a cloth and caught her uncle's eye again before he left.

'If you could just keep a watch on the bar for a while, I'll go and see that the spare room's ready for Mr

Tavener,' she said with deliberate formality, and especially since Corey was still close enough to over-hear.

Which he apparently did, for he immediately about-faced and sent her an extremely dry, extremely know-ing look, as if all too aware of her implied challenge.

'Since we'll be sharing the same quarters, don't you think it might be a little more appropriate if you used my first name?' he quizzed lazily.

Dale shrugged with feigned deprecation. 'I didn't want to be accused of taking liberties ... again,' she countered, sweetly tongue-in-cheek.

'Mmm, I can imagine,' he drawled with such a wry, crooked smile that she felt her knees grow weak. 'Then why don't you join us for a drink too, and we can get to know each other better, if that's what you would prefer?'

Actually, it was the last thing she wanted, and she shook her head quickly. 'No, thank you, I don't drink in the middle of the day,' she declined on a righteous-sounding note as she glanced pointedly at the beer can in his own hand.

'No, it gives her a headache,' explained Lester, unwittingly spoiling the whole effect—to Dale's morti-fication and Corey's obvious amusement. 'But you run along, lass, if you want to check out the room,' he went on amiably. 'Irwin and I'll see to the bar if anyone comes in.'

'Thank you,' she nodded briefly, and was almost to the door, and a hopeful return to serenity, before she spoke again. 'Will Mr—er—Corey be having his meals with us too, because I'll have to let Myra know?' She glanced from one to the other enquiringly.

'Of course he will,' spluttered her uncle, an uncomprehending frown for her apparent obtuseness adding further creases to his lined forehead. 'Where did you think he was going to eat?'

'Well, since he's a guest, I thought he might have preferred the guests' dining room,' she answered dulcetly, optimistically, and earned for herself an askance look from Corey that didn't exactly fill her with confidence.

Lester shook his head incredulously. 'Oh, naturally he doesn't! Corey's more like family than a guest. I would've thought you'd have seen that by now. In fact, I don't know what's come over you at all this morning, Dale,' he concluded in perplexed accents.

'Maybe she's got a touch of spring fever . . . brought on by all that talk about Kurt,' put forward Corey with decidedly suspect helpfulness.

'Could be,' Dale wasn't averse to conceding, facetiously, but she took her departure, before any other like comments could be made!

Spring fever, indeed! she grimaced as she turned down the passage leading to the kitchen. Neither Kurt nor the weather had anything to do with it—as he damned well knew!

Myra Robbins, the hotel's somewhat rotund cook, was already in the midst of preparing lunch when Dale arrived in the kitchen, her plump cheeks rosy from the heat given off by the huge black range behind her.

'There's a freshly made pot of tea on the stove if you'd like to help yourself,' she smiled on looking up to see who had entered.

'Sounds just what I need,' grinned Dale with feeling, and retrieved a mug from one of the capacious cupboards the room contained. After pouring the tea, she added sugar, and then perched companionably on one

corner of the table where the older woman was working. 'Lord, it's hot in here! I don't know how you stand
it,' she couldn't help exclaiming a few minutes later on
feeling beads of perspiration beginning to form at her
temples. 'Why don't you get Uncle Les to buy an
electric or a gas stove? It would make it much cooler,'
with a frowning glance for the old wood-burner.

Myra shrugged off handedly. 'Oh, the heat doesn't
worry me—I'm used to it—and I've been cooking on
this one for almost twenty years now. I figure I may as
well stick with the devil I know as start all over again
with one I don't,' she laughed ruefully. 'Besides, I
don't reckon it does too bad a job for all its age.'

'No, that's true,' Dale agreed willingly. Myra might
not have been a particularly inventive cook, but the
meals she did prepare were certainly tasty enough.
Then, absently staring into her mug, she broached the
subject which had been at the back of her mind ever
since she'd left the bar. 'Myra . . . you've always lived
in Karraparinka, haven't you?' she began diffidently.

'Well, all thirty-one years of my married life, I have,'
came the smiling reply.

'So you'd know Corey Tavener, then?'

'Corey?' The other woman stopped what she was
doing to look up in surprise. 'My word, I know Corey!
Tell me a person in this town who doesn't!' she added,
starting to laugh.

Dale took a hopefully casual mouthful of tea.
'And would you—er—know why he left?'

Instead of answering, Myra probed curiously, 'What
makes you ask? it's years since I've heard Corey's name
mentioned.'

'I—I was just wondering, that's all,' Dale offered
lamely. 'He booked into the hotel a while ago, and I . . .'

'Booked into this hotel?' Myra broke in to question.
'Well, yes. He . . .'

'Where is he now, then?' interrupted Myra again,
rinsing beetroot juice from her hands before drying
them on a paper towel. 'I'll have to go and say hello.
It's been such a long time since I've seen him, and he
always was a favourite of mine.'

As well as everyone else's—except hers—by the look
of things, thought Dale with some asperity. 'As far as
I know he's still on the verandah with my uncles and a
few others,' she relayed indifferently.

After Myra had left, Dale finished her tea slowly,
a feeling close to resentment overtaking her.
Somehow, she just knew that if Kurt had been gone
from Karraparinka for any length of time, his
return wouldn't have been greeted with the same
enthusiasm his stepbrother's had. Not that she had
ever seen anyone display any actual dislike of Kurt,
of course, but there was always a feeling of inexplicable reserve, a lack of acceptance almost, when he
was around.

Just like when her uncle had made that remark about
Kurt being in town more often now, the reminiscence
followed inexorably. There had been a certain nuance
of condemnation in his tone then too, and yet Corey
Tavener's apparent desertion of the property
altogether hadn't brought forth the slightest dis-
approval. The only one to have been censured, in fact,
had been herself for remarking on it! she recalled
moodily.

Washing her mug, Dale dried it and returned it to
the cupboard, her determination to find answers to all
she wanted to know gaining momentum as she headed
for the hotel's private quarters. Although she doubted

there would be many opportunities to question her uncles on the subject now that Corey was staying with them, Kurt would be another matter. He was coming in to town that evening to see her and she would be able to ask him then. If anybody knew the full facts concerning Corey Tavener, he should! she decided with no little satisfaction.

Dressed in a strapless, hydrangea blue sun-frock made of fine soft towelling, Dale was already waiting on the verandah when Kurt arrived a little after eight that night, and as he bounded up the short flight of steps to greet her she went forward to meet him happily. Twenty-nine-years old, tall and slim of build, he was a very attractive man with his sun-streaked blond hair and vivid blue eyes which, at that moment, were alight with pleasure as he bent to kiss her lightly.

From inside the hotel, a sudden concerted roar of laughter made itself heard above the general noise of voices and with a grin Kurt cocked his head in the direction of the bar. 'Sounds as if you've quite a roll up for midweek,' he commented.

'It's—er—something of a celebration, I gather,' Dale revealed drily.

'Oh?' He glanced curiously towards the bar again. 'What for?'

'Your stepbrother's return.'

The unexpectedness, if not bluntness, of her response caught him so unprepared that for a time all he could do was stare at her incredulously. 'You're joking!' he finally managed to exclaim on a hoarse note.

'No, he arrived this morning and booked into the

hotel for a couple of weeks,' she said with a smile for his astounded expression.

'You mean, Corey's really in Karraparinka?'

'Uh-huh,' she nodded. Then she laughed, 'Weren't you expecting him either?'

'God, no!' he ejaculated, but followed it with a half smile that seemed to cost him some effort. 'Although if all my thoughts hadn't been of you for the last few weeks, I suppose I'd have realised he'd show up sooner or later. I guess he's heard about his father, hasn't he?'

'Mmm, from a drover, I think he said.'

Kurt uttered a short, somewhat rueful laugh. 'It's amazing how word gets around, isn't it?' And catching hold of her hand in his, he started down the steps. 'Come on, let's go for a walk, shall we?'

It wasn't the suggestion Dale had been expecting and, in consequence, she held back a little, her violet-eyed gaze somewhat perplexed. 'Aren't you going in to see him?' she queried. From the sound of it, just about every other man in town had—and probably all the women too, if Myra's reaction had been any indication, she added with uncharacteristic waspishness.

'I—umm . . .' Pausing, he cleared his throat, a trifle uncomfortably, it seemed to Dale. 'Oh, there'll be plenty of time for me to see him later, I expect,' he shrugged excusingly. 'Tonight I came to see you.'

Allowing herself to be escorted down the steps, Dale accepted the indirect compliment silently, her thoughts still held by his unanticipated behaviour. 'Don't you like your stepbrother, Kurt?' she eventually just had to ask.

'Who, Corey?' He looked down at her in surprise. 'Yeah, he's okay. Most times we got on well enough.'

'Most times?' she picked up interestedly.

'Mmm, most times.' He refused to elaborate any further.

They crossed an intersecting street in sociable silence, but it was impossible for Dale not to voice another question. The matter intrigued her, despite herself.

'How long ago did he leave town?' she enquired in as impassive a tone as she could contrive.

Kurt exhaled a deep breath. A slightly impatient breath? Dale speculated. 'About eight years, I suppose.'

That was quite a time, as Myra had said. 'And this is the first occasion he's been back?'

'Yes.'

Short and to the point, and definitely impatient this time, she noted disappointedly. Yet there was still the most important question of all to come, and she couldn't stop now.

'Why did he leave?' she burst out hurriedly, before he could say anything that might forestall her.

Bringing them to a halt, Kurt combed a hand roughly through his hair, his features appearing strained in the moonlight. 'Look, I'd really rather not talk about it, if you don't mind,' he parried in a low, almost grating voice. 'What's it matter to you why he left? Or have you also fallen for that rakish charm of his, like every other female in town has at some time or another?' A bitter kind of resignation clouded his expression.

'Oh, don't be an idiot, of course I haven't!' she denied hastily. And in a humorous attempt to return to their normal uncomplicated footing, 'It's not only gentlemen who prefer blondes, you know!'

Fortunately, Dale could see some of the tenseness beginning to leave his face as his mouth curved ruefully.

'I'm sorry,' he apologised sincerely. 'I don't know what made me say something stupid like that.' He gave a smothered half laugh. 'The shock of discovering Corey had returned, I guess.'

'But if you get on all right together, why should it matter if he's back?' it was impossible for her not to ask.

With a sigh Kurt dropped his arm across her smooth, tanned shoulders and they continued walking. 'It's a long story and . . .' he smiled down at her contritely, 'I really don't want to talk about it. Do you mind?'

'Not if you don't want to,' she acceded, albeit not very honestly. 'The only reason I asked was because it seems I made a rather rash remark this morning about him having apparently deserted Tavener's Bridge, and the silence which followed was positively deafening! I just thought that if I knew a little more about the matter, I might have been able to avoid putting my foot in my mouth in the same way again.'

'You accused him of . . .?' Momentarily, his eyes closed in despair. 'Oh, hell, what did you have to go and say something like that for?'

'Because it seemed appropriate at the time. And if it's so wrong, I wish someone would just tell me *why*!' she wailed no less despondently.

Kurt drew in a sharp breath and then released it raggedly. 'It's wrong because Corey didn't leave Tavener's Bridge by choice. His father ordered him off the place—disowned him—and all the rest of the banishment bit!' he divulged in a seemingly uncontrollable rush.

'Oh, my God!' Dale clapped a hand to her mouth in dismay. 'No wonder Uncle Les looked so embarrassed! And Corey . . . I bet he could have choked me!' she groaned. 'Whatever did he do to make his father behave so drastically?'

'Does it really matter, after all these years?' he countered, looking a trifle ill at ease. 'No good can come of raking over old memories now.'

'I suppose you're right,' she agreed, since that was clearly what he wanted. 'But now I understand why everyone says Jack Tavener's as hard as nails. You'd have to be to turn your own son out like that, wouldn't you?'

The more so when that son was evidently well liked by the rest of the community, which surely must prove the presence of some redeeming qualities, she deduced pensively.

CHAPTER TWO

DALE was up early, as usual, the following morning in order to help Eileen, Myra's youngest teenage daughter, take round the guests' tea and biscuits. Not that there were many visitors staying at the hotel that week—the lull before the storm of the races, Eileen called it—but as she also always took cups in to her uncles as well she had to get up anyway.

Neither of her relatives showed much inclination for talking that morning, however—probably as a result of the unofficial celebrations the night before, Dale guessed amusedly—and she wondered if Corey Tavener would be as uncommunicative when she took in his tea. She had already noticed that Myra had made certain there was a cup set out for him.

A few minutes later, on receiving no answer to her knock on the door next to hers, she opened it a fraction and peered experimentally into the room. Corey, she saw, was still fast asleep, his hair tousled on to his forehead, his deeply bronzed chest contrasting starkly with the white sheet which covered him to the waist. Debating whether to wake him or not, Dale finally decided on the former because she wanted to speak to him anyway, and walking across the room she set the cup she was carrying down on his bedside table.

For a moment she stood looking at him—noting the even rise and fall of his chest, the length of his ebony lashes as they lay against his cheeks, the relaxed shape of his mouth which, even in sleep, had a captivating curve to it—and then, to her mortification, discovering herself to be trying to imagine what it would be like to wake each morning with such an attractive, sleek male animal beside her. With a dispelling shake of her head she hurried over to the French doors which led on to the side verandah and threw them wide open, wanting to feel the cool morning air on her heat-suffused cheeks, but unthinkingly flooding the room with sunlight as well.

'What in blazes do you think you're doing?' promptly came the drowsy enquiry from behind her.

'Waking you,' she half smiled with painstaking nonchalance as she turned back towards the bed.

'Thanks ... you've succeeded admirably,' he murmured drily. 'Now would you mind closing them again so I can go back to sleep?'

'But it's six o'clock,' she advised as if she had never been guilty of sleeping past that hour. 'And I've brought your tea,' indicating the cup beside the bed.

'Thank you,' even drier than before. 'But right at the moment all I want is some sleep.' He closed his eyes determinedly.

Dale's lips twitched involuntarily. 'Oh dear, have you got a headache?' she hazarded with false solicitude.

Abruptly, one topaz-gold eye flicked open to watch her with disconcerting directness. 'No, I do not have a headache,' he denied wryly. 'I just happen to be tired. I had three days of hot, hard driving to get here and, quite frankly, I could have done without last night's session at the end of it.'

'I see,' she nodded understandingly, her sympathy a little more genuine now, and retracing her steps she closed the doors in order to return the room to its previous dim state.

Approaching the bed again, she found both Corey's eyes shut and she chewed at the inside of her lip indecisively. She still hadn't said what she wanted to say to him, and the longer it stayed on her conscience the worse she knew she would feel about it. So . . .

'Corey?' she whispered tentatively, bending forward.

'Mmm . . .?' His response was somewhere between a sigh and a groan.

'I'm sorry, but there's something I wanted to speak to you about.'

'Can't it wait until later?' That was definitely groaned.

Since she suspected it would be quite some time before she managed to get him on his own again she shook her head negatively. 'No, I'm afraid it can't.'

'Oh, hell,' he muttered, eyes half opening reluctantly. 'Well, if you have to, you may as well be comfortable, and at the same time save me from breaking my neck looking up at you.' And, in a completely unexpected movement, he caught hold of her wrist and pulled her down on to the bed beside him.

'*Corey!*' Dale immediately protested in a mixture of outrage and surprise as she struggled to free herself from the steel band of his arm which was pinning her on her back. 'I only came to talk, not to keep you company! And—and what would my uncles think if they saw us?' on a rising note of panic at the thought. The bedroom door was still open as she'd left it.

Corey apparently had no such worries at the prospect, for he merely burrowed his head into the hollow between her throat and shoulder and mumbled indolently, irrelevantly, 'Hmm . . . you smell nice.'

Knowing he was still half asleep didn't, unfortunately, make Dale feel any better. In fact, the feel of his lips moving against her skin when he spoke had her already racing pulse pounding even harder, and she squirmed even more frantically to escape his grip. When this proved fruitless, she unwillingly had to concede that she was wasting her time and that her best chance of regaining her liberty was to say what she had to say as soon as possible, and then let him return to his slumbers as he so obviously desired.

'Corey, will you please listen to me for a minute?' she entreated with this plan in mind.

'I'm listening,' he nodded almost imperceptibly, but without removing his head from its disturbing resting place.

Dale licked at her soft lips and began hesitantly. 'Well, what I wanted to—to say, was . . . I'm very sorry for what I said yesterday about your—your having left Tavener's Bridge because you didn't care about it.'

When there was no answer forthcoming, Dale thought he must have gone back to sleep again, then she almost wished he had when his lips began moving against her suddenly ultra-sensitive skin once more.

'So who told you differently?' he questioned in a muffled voice.

Concerned at the disturbing way in which her senses were responding to his proximity, she replied without thinking, 'Kurt.'

'Oh?' With his head lifting slightly, he turned to look at her quizzically, his tone a fraction less drowsy now. 'When?'

'Does it matter?' she stalled, for fear that she had already disclosed too much.

A smile tilted his lips crookedly. 'When?' he repeated softly, insistently.

'L-last night,' she admitted grudgingly, throatily. That disarming smile had created havoc within her nervous system.

'You mean Kurt was in town last night?'

Dale nodded briefly.

'And, presumably, he knew I was too?' In a tone decidedly less sleepy this time.

She knew what he was getting at and nodded again, but on this occasion followed it with a rather jerkily defending, 'He said he expected to see you soon, anyway.' Which wasn't quite the way of it, but she thought it sounded better than what Kurt had actually said.

'So that's the way he means to play it, is it?' Corey half smiled wryly, but his meaning was lost to Dale. Amber eyes suddenly locked with wide, deepening violet. 'And did he also tell you why I was considered unacceptable at Tavener's Bridge?.

'No,' she was thankful to be able to report. 'He said he didn't want to talk about it.'

'No, he probably doesn't,' he concurred on what Dale suspected might have been a sardonic note.

'But you apparently thought he might have done,' she reminded him, curiosity getting the better of her.

'And?'

'Kurt also said the two of you were on good terms with each other . . . most times.'

Corey propped himself up on one elbow, his gaze intent as his head inclined sideways. 'Just what are you trying to say, my sweet?'

Dale shifted restively, her cheeks becoming flushed. 'Only that I—I was wondering if Kurt had anything to do with your—your . . .'

'Fall from grace?' he put in mockingly.

'Well . . . yes.'

'Then why don't you ask him whether he did or not?'

'I told you . . . apart from saying you hadn't left by choice, he wouldn't talk about it.'

'But you think I will?' He gave a short ironic laugh and, raising the arm which had been keeping her prisoner, caught her chin between thumb and forefinger. 'Right, now you've woken me up and made your apology. Why don't you just leave it at that, huh?'

'In other words, mind my own business!' she grimaced. Then, as a thought occurred to her, 'But, in a way, Kurt *is* my business.'

'Mmm, but I'm not,' he pointed out softly.

Dale averted her gaze selfconsciously. 'I wasn't meaning to imply that you were,' she defended in stiff accents, adding on a deliberately offhand note, 'I—I expect your wife would take great exception if I did.'

'Quite possibly,' he drawled laconically. 'If I had one.'

A strange feeling of relief beset her, and to overcome it, she broke free of his lighter though no less disturbing hold, and went on quickly as she was at last able to scramble off the bed and on to her feet.

'Well, in any case, that still wasn't what I meant to imply,' she denied again. And, with a shrug, 'I guess maybe I should have just left it at an apology, after all.'

Corey rolled on to his back and clasped his hands behind his head, the muscles in his arms bunching powerfully. 'I guess maybe you should,' he concurred wryly, lips tilting.

That he appeared to find something amusing in the situation had Dale's chin lifting challengingly higher.

'I'll let you go back to sleep, then, without any further interruptions,' she offered coolly, making for the door.

'Unfortunately, I doubt that will be possible ... now!'

The undisguised taunt had her drawing in an angry breath, although there was no sign of annoyance on her face when she half turned to look at him, just a mocking unconcern. 'Sorry,' she smiled facetiously. 'I'll see that it doesn't happen again, believe me!' And she proceeded to shut the door behind herself with a slam that should have woken the dead.

Since she rarely ate much for breakfast, Dale often joined Myra and Eileen in the kitchen for this meal, although even when she did so she normally took her uncles' meal to them. On this particular morning, however, she decided to exchange duties in this regard with the younger girl and while Eileen saw to their and Corey's requirements, she attended to the guests in the dining room. For the time being she considered it might have been judicious to give the unsettling Corey Tavener as wide a berth as possible.

Nevertheless, by the afternoon, and still not having seen the subject of her wayward thoughts again, she had ruefully come to the conclusion that, even though she was fully convinced she didn't want to talk *to* the man, she was still experiencing a perplexing wish to talk *about* him. So when she and one of her uncles were alone in the storeroom allocating space for the extra supplies that would be needed for the duration of the races, she promptly sought to satisfy the feeling of interest which assailed her and thereby, she hoped, put the man from her thoughts once and for all.

With her gaze concentrated on the bottles she was shifting, she began in as careless a tone as she could manage, 'Where's our guest gone today, Uncle Irwin? I haven't seen him since early this morning.'

'If you mean Corey, he's out at Tavener's Bridge,' came the just as casual reply.

Dale supposed she should have guessed that would be the case since his father's health had been the sole reason for Corey's return. She continued diligently with what she was doing. 'And what's his reception likely to be, do you think?'

'By whom?'

At that, she did partly turn round, her brows pulling together in a frown. 'Well, by his father, of course,' she explained in no little confusion.

'So you've already learned about that, have you? commented Irwin a shade ironically. 'I wonder who could have volunteered that information so eagerly.'

'It wasn't volunteered, and it wasn't eager either,' she denied defensively, sensing once again that unspoken criticism of Kurt. Her uncle knew as well as she did who would have been her informant. 'As a matter of fact, he didn't want to tell me at all.'

His shrewd brown eyes fixed her with an old-fashioned look. 'But you managed to persuade him otherwise?'

'Well, yes, something like that,' she admitted a trifle uncomfortably. For some obscure reason he made her feel guilty. 'Although only so I wouldn't go making another *faux pas* like I did yesterday morning.'

'Hmm.' He appeared to give the matter some thought. 'And is that all he told you?'

'Yes,' Dale confirmed quickly, positively. 'Though I really can't see why I shouldn't know what happened. I mean, it's apparent everyone else does.'

'Your only interest in the matter being so you can avoid future mistakes, hmm?'

'Of course! What other reason could there be?' Her violet eyes widened artlessly.

'An interest in the man himself, perhaps?' queried Irwin wryly, bluntly.

'Oh, no!' she disclaimed, her words punctuated by a light and, she hoped, convincing laugh. 'Dark-haired men have never done anything for me, and I'm quite content with Kurt. You know how they say opposites attract.' She fingered her own rich brunette curls significantly.

'You like Kurt because of the colour of his hair?' her uncle questioned incredulously.

Dale laughed again, but more genuinely on this occasion. 'Well, not entirely. He does have other attractive qualities.'

Irwin looked as if he was about to make some comment, then changed his mind and returned his attention to the cartons of beer he had been stacking. 'So what do you want to know about Corey?' he caught his niece off guard by suddenly asking.

Recovering swiftly, she immediately made the most of his offer. 'For a start, I'd like to know what caused that "By whom?" comment of yours, when I asked what his reception would be at Tavener's Bridge. I have a hunch it wasn't just an attempt to make everything appear normal . . . was it?' she probed watchfully.

Irwin's lips pursed in a thoughtful expression. 'No, not altogether, I suppose it wasn't,' he admitted with a sigh. 'Because unless I'm very much mistaken, Louise . . .' He stopped abruptly, exhaling a heavy breath. 'Look, lass, I'm not really sure I should be telling you all this. There was an awful lot of speculation about

the matter going on in town at the time, and after eight
years, who's to say what's the truth and what isn't? I
can only tell you what I think, and I might be completely wrong.'

'At least it would give me some idea of what
happened, though,' Dale put in hastily, nervous that
her source of information was about to dry up. 'And
... would I be right in assuming quite a few other
people think the same as you do?' remembering not
only Myra's, but also others' reactions when they
learnt of Corey Tavener's return.

'Probably,' was all he would concede, however.

'Oh, please, Uncle Irwin, you can't stop now!' she
was reduced to beseeching him. 'It's so frustrating
being just about the only person in Karra who doesn't
know the facts, and I promise not to let on to Corey
that you've told me, if that's what you're afraid of.'

'But that's just it, lass,' he half grimaced apologetically. 'There's very few actual facts I can pass on. Most
of it's pure supposition.'

'So you're backing out of telling me anything.' She
eyed him disappointedly, accusingly.

'No, I'm not backing out,' he denied in a testy voice,
and obviously not liking the connotation. 'It's just
that . . .'

'If you don't tell me, I shall ask everyone in town
until I find someone who will,' she broke in to threaten,
though not altogether seriously.

'Don't you dare!' Irwin roared, aghast, then, on
seeing the impish look on her face, relaxed with a rueful
smile. 'All right, all right, you got your message across.
Come hell or high water, you're going to find out!' He
sighed defeatedly.

Dale rewarded him with a captivating grin and

prompted, 'You were saying, about Mrs Tavener . . .?'

'That I wouldn't be at all surprised if she wasn't particularly overjoyed to see Corey again,' he relayed flatly.

'Oh?' Her winged brows peaked interestedly. 'Corey and his stepmother don't get along?'

'W-e-ll,' he lingered over the word contemplatively, 'I don't know that I'd go so far as to say that exactly. On the surface, at least, they seemed to, and yet at the same time, Louise was always so preoccupied with her own sons' welfare—and what she considered to be their entitlement—that Les and I often wondered if all was as well between her and Corey as it might have been.' He gave a wry laugh of remembrance. 'Of course, the fact that her stepson—even at an early age—was as independent as they come didn't really endear him to her. Louise likes to be the guiding force behind her menfolk, so when she found she not only couldn't control her new husband as she would have wished, but that Corey wasn't about to meekly succumb to her every command either, it didn't make for a particularly auspicious beginning.'

Dale's head tipped to one side enquiringly. 'How old was Corey when his father remarried?'

'About fourteen, as near as I can recall.'

'His own mother had died, had she?'

'Mmm, a couple of years or so before.'

'What was she like?'

'Who, Yvette?' He suddenly smiled, his expression becoming reminiscent. 'Oh, she was a lovely little thing, with masses of fiery red curls covering her head, and enormous brown eyes. It always used to make everyone smile to see her and Black Jack together, because he's such a giant of a man and she looked so tiny beside him, but if she'd asked him to cut off his legs to bring him down to her size, I reckon he would've done it. He truly worshipped the ground that girl walked on, and in all the years I've known him she was the only one he ever showed a softer side of his nature to.'

'Not even to his own son? Or—or his second wife and his stepsons?' she frowned sceptically.

Her uncle uttered a disparaging snort. 'Especially not to his own son,' came the startling revelation which had Dale's frown deepening confusedly.

'But why?'

'Because as far as Jack Tavener was concerned, his son was the cause of his wife's death.'

'How?' she demanded on an incredulous note.

'By having been born,' he half smiled sadly. 'You see, unfortunately, Yvette was as fragile as she looked—too fragile for the life out here, especially in those days—and she had such a bad time with Corey's birth that, afterwards, she was even more delicate than she had been before. She just seemed to contract one illness after another, with each one draining a little bit more out of her until, in the end, when she came down with pneumonia she had no strength left to fight it at all.'

'That's tragic, of course,' Dale owned sympathetically. 'But to blame your own son for it when it must have been just as heartbreaking for him as well is inhuman! If he thought so much of his wife, perhaps Mr Tavener should have considered the state of her health before deciding to have a child in the first place, and if it was that hard for her out here, why didn't he move somewhere else?'

Irwin shrugged helplessly. 'Yes, well, I'm inclined

to agree with your sentiments with regard to Corey,' he confessed. 'Nevertheless, I must give the man his due concerning Yvette. He wasn't prepared to risk the dangers of her having a child, that was all her doing. As it was for staying here. I know for a fact Jack wanted to take her away, but she wouldn't hear of it. She loved the Gulf country almost as much as he did, even though the conditions and climate were too tough for her.'

'I see,' she nodded meditatively, forgetting to make even a pretence of keeping on with the work now. 'It sounds as if Corey's had a raw deal from his father since birth, and yet to look at him he doesn't give the impression of having had what must have been a somewhat dispiriting childhood, does he? I mean, there's no obvious chip on the shoulder, or anything like that. Quite the opposite, really, I would have said.'

'Mmm, and contrarily, maybe he has his father to thank for that, because there's more than a little of Jack Tavener's stubbornness in his son, believe me!' stated her uncle drily. 'Apart from a few wild years, I think Corey's come through it as well as he has because he just plain refused to let his father break him, no matter what.'

'A few wild years?' she repeated quizzically.

'Oh, yes.' He gave voice to a wry chuckle of laughter. 'For a while there after finishing his schooling, young Corey had himself quite a reputation. He'd be in anything, up to everything, and he didn't have to go looking for feminine company either ... it came looking for him.' His face suddenly sobered. 'Regretfully, though, I've always figured it was that reputation which made it so easy for Jack to believe the worst of him at the last.'

'Which is when he did . . . what?' Now they were approaching the heart of the matter!

'Supposedly got a girl into trouble, then declined point-blank to marry her,' Irwin relayed baldly. 'And that's something which just isn't done in a town this size where everyone knows everyone else, and particularly when the girl happens to be the daughter of one of your father's oldest acquaintances.'

Dale absorbed the information thoughtfully, unwilling for a moment to commit herself either way. 'You said, "supposedly"?' she probed on a curious note.

'There are a lot of people who don't believe Corey was responsible.'

'Including you and Uncle Lester?' she surmised from his tone.

'Including Les and myself,' he confirmed with a nod. 'You see, even with his reputation, Corey was still one of the most liked blokes in town—as you could probably tell from his reception yesterday—because whatever strife he may have got himself into, there was never any attempt to dodge whatever consequences eventuated. So when his father gave him the option to either marry the girl or get out, and he promptly left, it just didn't fit in with what everyone knew of his character.'

'Did he deny it, though?'

'No,' he sighed. 'And that, probably more than anything, is what no one could understand.'

'They didn't happen to think it may have been a sign of guilt?' she suggested a trifle sardonically.

'Of course that occurred to them,' he returned in mild exasperation. 'The more so because no one thought Wanda was the type of girl to make such a

claim unless there was some basis of truth in it,
but . . .'

'Wanda?' she broke in to repeat. 'You mean, Wanda
Gilchrist was the girl involved? And that young
Reuben is Corey's child?' Kurt had introduced her to
the young woman at last month's dance held in the
Shire Hall, and she often saw blond-headed Reuben
passing the hotel on his way to and from the local
primary school.

Although, now she came to think of it, Kurt had
been rather cool and offhand with his introduction.
Nor had he spoken very favourably about Wanda afterwards, which had surprised her at the time because
she'd found her to be quite pleasant, if a little tense.
Now she knew the reason both of them had acted the
way they did. Wanda had been the cause of Kurt's
stepbrother having to leave town.

'Yes, Wanda Gilchrist was the girl involved, but no,
I don't believe Reuben is Corey's child.' Irwin's
decisive-sounding voice snapped her back to the present. 'As I was saying, even though it was Wanda
making the claim . . .'

'Since it's a male-dominated community, you
naturally all took the man's part . . . as always,' she
interrupted again, but caustically now rather than sardonically.

His mouth thinned with exasperation. 'Then perhaps you might care to explain why most of the women
were of the same mind too?' he requested in victori-
ously mocking accents.

'No doubt because women, foolishly, have always
had a soft spot for a rogue,' she retorted drily. 'Also,
they tend to be more suspicious of others of their own
sex than men are in such matters.'

'With good reason, maybe?' he quipped meaningfully.

'Not always, no,' she disallowed with a grudging smile. 'And in this instance, since there was no denial ...'

'No admission either,' he was quick to insert.

'Isn't that implied when it's not denied?' she retaliated just as rapidly.

'Not always, no,' he used her own words against her. Then, returning his attention to the cartons he had been piling against one wall, he shrugged, 'Anyway, whether you think Corey was or wasn't responsible, you know as much as I do now.'

'Not quite,' Dale disagreed with a diffident lift of one shoulder. 'Earlier, you said something about Louise Tavener being preoccupied with what she considered to be her sons' entitlement. What did you mean by that?'

Irwin moved a crate of bottles out of his way and went on with what he was doing. 'Louise always hated the idea of Corey having a prior claim on Tavener's Bridge. Since she was now Jack's wife, she thought Kurt and Karl should have first rights to the property.'

'Surely his father didn't accede to her wishes?' she gasped incredulously. It was unbelievable that anyone could be so coldbloodedly ambitious! Or was it avaricious?

'He wouldn't want to have done,' her uncle suddenly guffawed loudly, and with more than a hint of disparagement in his tone, she noted. 'Those two couldn't run a cattle property if their lives depended on it! No, Jack's always known Corey was the only one capable of keeping Tavener's Bridge going once—if—he ever lets go of the reins.'

Dale bristled indignantly on Kurt's behalf. 'Now *you're* not being fair!' she charged hotly. 'Kurt's been doing a tremendous amount of work since Mr Tavener's been ill. So has Karl. And—and if they maybe haven't learnt as much as they should, then perhaps that's their stepfather's fault for not having taught them!'

'Or theirs, for not having the nous to learn?' he countered none too subtly.

'They have learnt!' she insisted. 'Don't forget, it's been harder for them than it was for Corey in that regard. He at least was born on a property. They weren't.'

'And Kurt's still liable to lose his bearings if he strays too far from the beaten track.' Irwin's lip curled derisively.

'Oh, he is not!'

'Isn't he? That's not what I hear.'

'From whom?' she demanded.

'Those people who know,' he informed her noncommittally. 'And it's no use you glaring so fiercely at me either, young lady,' with a wry smile, 'because that doesn't alter the facts in the slightest. No matter how Kurt, or you, might like to pretend otherwise, I'm sorry to say both he and his brother are like fish out of water on a cattle station, and I'm surprised Louise didn't admit as much years ago.'

'Why Mrs Tavener, in particular?' Dale frowned, momentarily diverted.

'Because, with Corey gone, I suspect she went back to hoping Kurt or Karl, or both, would inherit the place some day, after all, and in order for that to have a chance of happening they had to stay around.'

Dale shook her head in bewilderment. 'I still think you're wrong where Kurt's concerned. He's never seemed out of place here to me.'

'Mmm, but then you're prejudiced, aren't you, lass?' he teased gently.

'Well, aren't you too . . . against him?' she couldn't help but remark. Her eyes contained a hurt expression as they held his. 'Neither you nor Uncle Les like him, do you, Uncle Irwin?'

He shrugged dispassionately. 'It's not for us to like or dislike him. It's how you feel about him that matters.'

'That doesn't answer my question!'

With a sigh he placed his hands on her shoulders, his glance apologetic as he met her amethyst gaze. 'Look, love, it's obvious I've upset you already with all this talk of Kurt, and I'm sorry. Les and I didn't want to interfere in your affairs, we didn't think we had a right to, but if you're so determined to know, then I'm afraid the answer is, no, we do not feel particularly favourably disposed towards him.'

Just as she had guessed! 'But why not?' she went on doggedly. 'And it's not only you and Uncle Les who feel that way either, is it? I've noticed whenever Kurt's around there always seems to be a holding back, a feeling almost that is presence is merely being suffered, but I've never been able to discover the reason for it. What on earth has he done to apparently put everyone's backs up this way? Or is it just that in towns the size of Karraparinka, you have to have lived here all your life before you're accepted as one of the community?'

'I wouldn't say that. You've been accepted, haven't you?' One iron-grey eyebrow rose explicitly.

'I suppose so,' she nodded thoughtfully. She had certainly experienced nothing but friendliness to date. 'Then why not Kurt too?' she just had to ask again.

Irwin gave vent to a resigned sigh, realising she wasn't going to let the matter drop until she'd received the answer she wanted. 'You really want to know?' he grimaced with a rather sardonic inflection. And after her emphatic nod of confirmation, 'Okay, then I'll tell you. As you so rightly surmised, that young man does rub people the wrong way, and for a number of reasons. For a start, he has the unfortunate idea of believing that just because he lives on the biggest property in the district, that also makes him the biggest man in the district, and although he may not exactly be the original bushman,' with dry emphasis, 'out at Tavener's Bridge, he likes to play the part whenever he's in town! As well as that, even though his grasp of pastoral practices is minimal, that doesn't stop him from criticising those far more knowledgeable than himself and telling them where he considers they're going wrong and what they should do to rectify the matter. In other words,' he half smiled ruefully, 'he doesn't go down very well with the local inhabitants because he's, quite frankly, nothing short of a pain in the neck!'

The disclosure came as something of a shock to Dale and she frowned. 'I've never heard him offering advice or—or anything to anyone,' she put forward doubtfully.

'Probably because when he's with you, he has other things besides cattle on his mind,' he laughed drily.

'You'd rather I wasn't quite so friendly with him, though, wouldn't you?' she deduced without too much effort.

Dropping his hands from her shoulders, her uncle then raised one again in order to rub the tips of his fingers across his forehead. 'Oh, hell, lass, what kind of a question is that to ask?' he despaired. 'You can only judge as you find, and if you find him likeable— well, who knows . .? Maybe you're just what he needs to make him come to his senses.' He paused, smiling encouragingly. 'All I ask is that you don't allow our opinion of him to distort your judgment, and that you remember he's not the only pebble on the beach.'

Raising herself up on tiptoe, Dale placed a fond kiss against his leathery cheeks. 'I'll keep it in mind,' she promised softly.

It was just on dusk by the time they eventually finished in the storeroom, and as Irwin made his way towards the office, Dale continued on to their quarters. Before helping to serve dinner she wanted to shower away the dust she seemed to have accumulated during the afternoon.

Once in her room she began selecting the clothes she would wear, but as a slight noise from the verandah outside floated in through the open doors, she stopped what she was doing and went to have a look. Apart from her uncles and herself, no one usually came around to this part of the rambling, two-storied building.

To her surprise, as she stepped outside, she found Corey seated in a cane chair with his long legs propped up on the wooden railing which encompassed the verandah, and a glass of amber liquid in his hand. On a small table beside him stood a partially used bottle of whisky and a well-used ashtray.

'I didn't realise you were back,' she said by way of an opening, and then berated herself inwardly for sounding so inane. How would she have known he had returned?

Corey's eyes swept over her in a raking glance. 'I gather you know where I've been, though,' he stated on an ironic note.

'Y-yes,' she faltered, unsure whether to advance or retreat, but finally settling herself against the railing not too far distant from his chair, and giving a light, nervous laugh. 'You should know you couldn't keep something like that a secret in Karra.'

'Hmm.' Lifting his glass, he took a swallow and then sat studying its remaining contents in silence.

In turn, Dale watched his expression intently, not knowing quite what to make of his attitude as yet. 'So how is your father, then?' she prompted gently.

Except for one brief upward look of glittering intensity, his gaze continued its seemingly fascinated contemplation of his glass. 'I really couldn't say for sure. I didn't get to see him,' he relayed with a wry twist to his firmly moulded lips.

'You didn't get to . . .!' She broke off with a sharp intake of breath, her violet eyes staring at him confusedly. 'Why ever not?'

He uttered a short humourless laugh, but instead of replying, countered sardonically, 'Have you ever had the feeling you've been had, angel?'

Dale shrugged helplessly. 'Sometimes, I guess,' she owned in a throaty voice. Something had obviously gone wrong today. Something that had put a smouldering glow in the depths of his normally teasing eyes, and which now had her eyeing him warily. If she had thought him darkly dangerous when they had first met, it was nothing as to how he appeared now—but in a completely different manner. 'What makes you ask?'

she continued in the same whispery tone.

'No particular reason,' he denied, and draining his glass swiftly, immediately poured a refill. 'Forget it.'

It was the perfect time for Dale to make her exit, but somehow she just couldn't bring herself to take that first step towards leaving. Instead, she inclined her head in the direction of the table. 'That isn't going to help you know,' she commented tentatively.

'You think I've had too much already?' he questioned, harshly mocking.

'N-o.' She shook her head slowly, refusing to drop her gaze beneath the hard challenge of his. 'I think you're so damned furious, you're using it as a substitute because you can't do what you really feel like doing.'

'Which is?'

The beginnings of a rueful smile pulled at the corners of her mouth, then abruptly disappeared again. 'Slit someone's throat, I think.'

'And just what makes you so knowledgeable when it comes to my behaviour, hmm?' Corey taunted as he swung his feet to the floor and rose upright, all in the same lithe action.

Dale took two apprehensive steps backward. 'I didn't say I was,' she disputed, nervously catching at her bottom lip with even white teeth. 'You asked me a question and I answered it, that's all' Then, when he didn't immediately reply, she took her courage in both hands and ventured to ask, 'Corey, what happened at Tavener's Bridge today?'

All of a sudden the mockery which previously had been directed towards her now seemed to be turned inwards. 'Nothing more than I should have expected,' he half laughed derisively.

'Meaning?' she prompted hesitantly.

'Meaning, I've been keeping my own counsel since I was twelve, angel, so I guess I'm out of practice when it comes to sharing confidences,' he advised wryly. 'How about you wait and let Kurt tell you all the details, huh? He probably wouldn't take kindly to hearing I'd stolen his thunder by telling you first, anyway.'

'You're saying you're not my concern again, is that it?'

'It seems safest.' He reached out a large brown hand to cup her chin and ensure that her heart-shaped face remained tilted up to his. 'Or I might suddenly decide to return the compliment, and make you *my* concern.' His mouth curved ruefully. 'And that, I don't doubt, Kurt definitely wouldn't take kindly.'

'He doesn't own me.' Her declaration of independence was out before Dale could forestall it, and a rosy selfconscious colour invaded her smooth cheeks. Heavens, maybe he was right and she really was suffering from spring fever, after all! That had been tantamount to asking him to take an interest in her, she realised in dismay. 'No one does,' she now added hurriedly in a belated attempt to modify the remark.

One of his brows quirked ironically higher than the other. 'From what I hear, Kurt appears to think otherwise.'

'Then he's taking too much for granted. I—I enjoy his company, but there's nothing binding between us,' she felt obliged to point out, then immediately wished she hadn't on seeing the deepening expression that closed over his good-looking features.

'Neither will there be, if I have anything to do with it,' he predicted in a warm, resonant voice as he bent unexpectedly to claim her lips with his own in a burning demand.

Dale's world promptly began pitching wildly. The mastery of his mouth was making her senses reel and her pulse quicken tempestuously, and although she tried not to respond, her lips seemed to have a will of their own as they unreservedly returned the pressure of his and, willingly parting, capriciously savoured new delights. Where Kurt's mouth was soft and persuasive when he kissed her, his stepbrother's was firm and possessive, and the latter was a combination she found herself helpless to resist. That she also didn't want to, did give her some moments of alarm, however.

What kind of a fool was she? No matter how attractive he was, the man was still a known womaniser with a reputation already for 'loving and leaving'. Naturally he was experienced at making love! By all accounts, he'd had quite some considerable practice! Wanda Gilchrist could attest to that, couldn't she? No doubt that girl had found him irresistible too, but that wasn't what she wanted for herself, was it ... a temporary affair? To Dale's relief that thought, above all others, finally gave her the resolve to break away from his overwhelming touch.

'Corey ... don't!' she partly begged, partly protested, unsteadily. 'You make me feel disloyal to Kurt, and—and ...' remembering his last remark, 'I don't want to be a pawn in any game you're planning to play against him.'

'Who said I was intending to do either?' he quizzed on a heavy note.

'You did,' she reminded him jerkily. The look in his honey-coloured eyes refused to allow her breathing to resume its normal even cadence. 'You said there would never be anything binding between Kurt and myself if you could prevent it.'

'But not because I'm playing any game, angel,' he corrected softly.

'Then why?'

'Why does a man kiss a girl?' he qualified in whimsical drawl. 'Usually because he feels like it . . . because she attracts him. And you, my sweet, are very attractive.'

Dale drew in a deep, calming breath. 'As well as handy?'

'Just what's that supposed to mean?'

She held his watchful gaze valiantly. 'Your reputation precedes you, Corey, but I've no intention of providing the means for you to casually entertain yourself while you're in Karraparinka.' There, she'd said it! It was best to get it out in the open so there could be no misunderstanding.

'Is that so?' His eyes darkened with mockery. 'Well, apart from the fact that I wasn't aware I'd asked you to provide such entertainment, that still wasn't quite the impression you gave a few minutes ago.'

Dale could feel her face going scarlet. 'That—that was a mistake,' she declared in a strangled voice. 'A momentary . . .'

'Oh, don't give me that!' he cut in roughly. 'That was no damned mistake, and you know it!' Abruptly, his mood gentled again and his mouth tilted wryly. 'The same as you know you're no more unaware of me, my sweet, than I am of you.'

Recognising that he spoke nothing more than the truth, she didn't even attempt to deny it, but in her anxiety to keep him at a distance she rushed into unpremeditated speech.

'I'm still no Wanda Gilchrist, though,' she asserted desperately.

A muscle leapt at the side of Corey's jaw, his entire aspect changing as he fixed her with an ominous, narrow-eyed glance that sent slivers of ice racing down her spine. 'What did you say?' he rapped out grimly.

Dale swallowed convulsively. 'I said I was n-no Wanda Gilchrist,' she repeated in an almost inaudible stammer.

'Well, that's a relief!' His words slashed at her with bitter, biting sarcasm. 'Although whether Kurt thinks the same is another matter, of course, isn't it?'

'I don't know what you mean,' she whispered tremulously.

'No? Well, if you want answers, do me a favour and try asking Kurt for a change, huh?' he suggested tauntingly as he swept up the glass and bottle from the table and began heading for his room. At the open doorway he turned back. 'Just don't ever come questioning me again, okay?'

Dale nodded mutely, suddenly conscious of an inexplicable feeling of loss and longing to go after him, but too frightened of the consequences to dare. Besides, she attempted to console herself, this was how she had wanted it . . . wasn't it?

CHAPTER THREE

SINCE Corey didn't explain to Dale's uncles either the reason for his not having seen his father—at least not in her presence—it wasn't until two evenings later when Kurt came into town that she was in a position to discover just what had occurred at Tavener's Bridge that particular day.

At the time she was helping behind the bar with both her uncles for, being a Saturday, it was their busiest night of the week when all the ringers and station hands from the surrounding properties made their weekly trip in to Karraparinka, looking for one kind of entertainment or another.

Across the street the open-air cinema also had a full house, and was the cause of Kurt's presently somewhat disgruntled expression as he slumped rather than sat on his stool at one end of the bar and leant back against the wall.

'Why do you have to work Saturday night of all nights?' he complained immediately she returned to him after fulfilling another spate of orders. 'You don't usually, and I thought we'd go to the movies tonight.'

'I'm sorry,' Dale smiled apologetically. 'But as you can see,' waving a hand to indicate the packed premises, 'there's far too many in here tonight for Uncle Les and Uncle Irwin to handle on their own. In any case,' she pulled a rueful moue, 'I've already seen the film they're showing, and it really wasn't all that good.'

Unfortunately, that didn't appear to make him feel any less dissatisfied. 'I still would've liked the chance to at least judge for myself,' he grumbled.

'Well, you could go across and see it and then come back here afterwards, if you like,' she proposed equably. 'We probably won't be so rushed later, and it will be easier for us to talk.'

'Maybe, but you needn't think I'm . . .'

'Sorry, I'll be back in a minute,' she interrupted with another regretful look on seeing someone else trying to catch her attention, and had to hurry away once more before he could finish. When she was finally able to return again, some considerable time later as it so happened, she half grimaced expressively and sent him an enquiring glance.

'Now, what was it you were saying?'

'It doesn't matter, it wasn't important,' he shrugged dismissively, his blue gaze not really holding hers but roaming over the crowded room instead, and resting longest on a large group consisting solely of men sitting around a table near one of the three open doorways. His mouth proceeded to shape a little bitterly. 'I see it hasn't taken long for my stepbrother to re-gather his circle of cronies around him, though.'

Of their own volition, Dale's eyes swung in Corey's direction to dwell meditatively on his rugged figure before she could determinedly drag them back to the man in front of her.

'He did invite both *you* and Karl to join them,' she reminded him with slight emphasis. That had been when the two brothers first entered the bar, and although Kurt might have declined, twenty-five-year-old Karl had accepted willingly.

'Mmm, knowing I never did have much in common with any of those fellers.'

'Karl seems to be doing all right,' she shrugged.

'Probably by agreeing with everything Corey says. My young brother always did tend to hero-worship him,' Kurt disclosed sardonically, and in Dale's estimation, perhaps a trifle jealously too.

Not that she was given the opportunity to pursue her line of thought—even had she considered it prudent to do so—because she had to attend to another customer requiring service, and when she came back this time she had already decided to change the topic—slightly.

'As a matter of fact, I heard that Corey was out at Tavener's Bridge the other day,' she began conversationally. 'Did you see him?'

Kurt hunched one shoulder offhandedly. 'Only for a few minutes. He wasn't there long.'

'Not even long enough to see his father, as I understand it.' Dale left the remark hanging hopefully in the air as she went about refilling the empty spaces in the fridge behind her.

'Oh?' His eyes narrowed curiously. 'Who told you that?'

'Why, isn't it true?' she countered in lieu of answering.

'Yes, it's true,' he confirmed briefly. 'But I'd still be interested to learn how you came to know about it.'

Dale shut the fridge door and schooled her features into remaining only casually concerned. 'Well, it was Corey himself, actually,' she owned lightly. 'When Uncle Irwin told me he'd gone out to the property— Corey, that is—the next time I saw him I naturally asked how his father was.'

'Whereupon he said . . .?'

'He didn't know, as he hadn't seen him.'

'Because?' Kurt waited expectantly.

'Because . . . nothing,' she returned wryly. 'He didn't give a reason.'

He gave a short sardonic laugh tinged with grudging admiration. 'I guess I should have known. Corey always was tight-lipped when it came to personal matters.'

Considering all the circumstances, Dale didn't exactly find that surprising. 'So why didn't he see his father, then?' she quizzed in a blunter fashion than she had intended.

'For Pete's sake!' Kurt exclaimed, sounding irritated. 'Don't tell me we're going to spend another evening talking about my stepbrother!'

'Well, aside from the fact that you happened to mention him first, just what do you mean, *another* evening talking about him?' Dale queried indignantly, giving vent to a little exasperation herself.

His expression became distinctly satirical. 'I thought that's all we did the last time I came in to see you.'

'Oh, don't exaggerate,' she chided with a half laugh. 'If we spoke about him for five minutes that would have been the limit. Anyway, since you never mentioned having a stepbrother, isn't it only to be expected that I'll ask a few questions now that he's suddenly turned up out of the blue? Especially when, to all apparent intents and purposes, he's only come all this way in order to see his father, then doesn't get to do anything of the kind after all, when he drives out to Tavener's Bridge.'

'Yes, well, my mother didn't think it was advisable,' he relayed abruptly, and took a long swallow from the can before him.

'Not advisable?' she echoed, a frown descending on to her normally smooth forehead. 'For whatever reason?'

'Because she didn't want Black Jack upset, of course,' he retorted in a blustering voice. 'He still hasn't completely recovered, you know, and the shock of Corey appearing from nowhere like that could have had a serious effect on him. Besides, after that last blow-up they had, Corey always swore he'd never return to Karraparinka.'

'Maybe he wouldn't have if his father hadn't become ill,' she surmised slowly, absently, not knowing quite what to make of the almost peevish tone in which Kurt had made his last disclosure. The other night he had merely given the appearance of being a little discomfited by his stepbrother's return, and that had been surprising enough, but now, for some equally unknown and just as strange reason, that feeling seemed to have turned to one of resentment. With a clearing shake of her head she tried concentrating on something a little, but only a very little, more tangible. 'So what's Corey supposed to do now? Wait until your mother's broken the news gently before attempting to see his father again?' In actual fact, she couldn't really see why Louise Tavener hadn't been able to do that two days ago while Corey was at the property.

'She'll have to, I suppose,' he allowed indifferently.

Even deeper furrows began creasing Dale's forehead now. 'You mean, she doesn't *want* to?'

'Whether she does or not, in the end it won't be her choice to make,' Kurt laughed harshly. 'Corey's no fool. He's well aware that all he has to do is wait her out.'

'I don't follow you.' She stared at him confusedly,

becoming more and more perplexed by the minute.

'The races,' he elucidated sardonically. 'My step-father would have to be either dead or unconscious before he'd miss those, and Corey knows that as well as anyone.'

'I see,' she nodded, thankful that at least one point had been satisfactorily explained. 'But why would your mother want to delay telling him in the first place? It seems awfully'—about to say malicious, she judiciously altered it to, 'unfair to me. Doesn't it to you?' she added searchingly after a slight pause.

'Perhaps in some ways,' he owned, although not overly enthusiastically. 'But since she was a hospital matron before they married, I guess she knows what's best for her husband. After all, just because the prodigal son's deigned to return, that's no guarantee his father will want to see him, is it?' A hint of rancour began creeping into his voice again.

'Not even after an absence of eight years?' Dale exclaimed incredulously.

'What's the length of time got to do with it? The circumstances haven't altered. Anyway, Karl and I are the ones who've done all the work on the place ever since he left.' He obviously couldn't restrain himself from airing his grievance.

So that was what had caused his sudden change in attitude. Just as her uncle had forecast. 'You and your mother are worried that if Corey and his father settle their differences, then Corey might reclaim his inheritance, as it were, now that he's here?' she hazarded as impassively as she could.

'I didn't say that!' he denied hotly. 'I merely said it's quite possible my stepfather may not wish to see him.'

'How would you know, unless someone tells him his son's here?'

'I told you, he'll find out at the races, even if not before.'

'In other words, he's fit enough to make the journey in here, but not fit enough for Corey to be allowed to see him, is that it?' she proposed on an uncontrollably sardonic note.

'Since we know what his reaction will be to one, but not to the other, then yes, I suppose you could say that,' he retorted tersely.

Had she misjudged him? speculated Dale inwardly as she went about serving once more. He sounded sincere enough, and yet . . .

'What makes you think it will be less of a shock for him to suddenly come face to face with his son in town rather than at home?' she couldn't help quizzing as soon as the opportunity was afforded her.

From his demeanour it was clear Kurt's patience was rapidly running out. 'Because, in the meantime, we'll have been able to drop a few hints in his ear!' he snapped.

What kind of hints? Dale promptly found herself wondering tartly, and pulled herself up with a start. Wasn't she the one being unfair now? For all she knew they might have been intending to do their very best by Corey. Even though Kurt had as good as implied his mother wouldn't have said anything to her husband if she hadn't known Corey could out-wait her and see his father at the races? asked a disquieting voice somewhere inside her head.

With a sigh she determinedly thrust the thought into the darkest recesses of her mind. When all was said and done, it *was* a family matter, and Corey wasn't her concern . . . as he had so succinctly pointed out twice now!

'Yes—well—would you like another beer?' She seized on the chance to seek neutral ground after watching Kurt efficiently drain the remainder of the contents of his can, and on receiving his concurring nod, set off for the farthest fridge where his preferred brand of ale was stored.

About to open the door, Dale caught the sound of angry voices raised above the general level of noise, followed by the clatter of a chair being overturned, and she quickly dashed round the end of the bar and the group of men lining its length.

Nearly everyone was on their feet now, she noticed, and either looking outside or beginning to move on to the verandah, and she began pushing between them urgently. When she was almost to the doorway a hand wrapped itself inescapably around her upper arm and abruptly halted her progress.

'Just where do you think you're going?' demanded Corey roughly. 'A fight's no place for you.'

'Maybe not, but they're going to wreck all the furniture if someone doesn't stop them soon!' she retorted as she heard another chair suffer the same fate as the first, and then winced involuntarily at the solid crunching sound of bone striking against bone.

'Well, that person isn't likely to be you, that's for sure!' he declared in the same peremptory tone. 'According to what I hear it's a grudge fight that's been a long time coming, and it's best to let them get it out of their systems once and for all. Besides, you can bet your life one of your uncles has already sent for the police.' The corners of his mouth crooked wryly. 'This isn't the first fight there's been in this pub, you know.'

'I'm well aware of that, but usually it's only scuffles that never amount to anything,' she replied worriedly, attempting to extricate herself from his grasp. 'Not like this, where someone's liable to really get hurt.' She shuddered again as another punishing blow landed. 'Surely somebody can stop them, or at least do something!'

'Don't worry, they'll stop immediately one of the boys in blue shows, and more than likely very thankfully too,' he advised ironically. 'So why don't you steer well clear of it and go back to the bar with your uncles, hmm?' Releasing her, he propelled her gently but resolutely towards the back of the room.

Although Dale's first inclination was to rebel against such arbitrary treatment, on noticing she was the only one present who appeared to be at all anxious over the proceedings—indeed, her uncles were only displaying a cursory interest—she eventually made no protest but did as had been suggested. Presumably, having obviously gone through similar situations before, her relatives knew what they were doing.

A couple of minutes later, coinciding with the arrival of the local police sergeant, Dale observed wryly, everyone had resumed their previous positions, and even the two combatants—complete with a closing eye apiece, bloodied noses and split lips—were leaning innocently against the wall by the time the uniformed figure entered the bar.

Built on the lines of an all-in wrestler, Bill Cooper was a well-respected man with a whimsical sense of humour that had stood him in good stead as the law's representative in Karraparinka for the past fifteen years. His position made him an integral part of the community, and as a result, he also knew all those who were members of it.

Now, as he moved through the crowded room, his shrewd blue eyes surveyed the scene leisurely, and finally came to rest on the two worse-for-wear ringers.

'I'm glad to see you fellers in town and so full of energy, because I need volunteers,' he informed them drily. 'You know the country round Andiah way, don't you?'

Squinting, they nodded ruefully.

'What d'you need volunteers for, Bill?' called someone curiously.

'Yeah, what's on at Andiah?' asked another.

'One of Arnold White's little nippers went missing this afternoon,' was the heavily divulged answer. 'It came over the radio a few moments ago. They've asked for volunteers to make up a search party to begin looking again at first light tomorrow.'

'Hell, that's no good!' ejaculated Ferris Broadbent with a frown, expressing everyone's thoughts. 'Which is the one that's lost?'

'Young Mickey,' relayed the sergeant.

'You should've guessed, Ferris,' half laughed the man next to him wryly. 'That kid's never stopped wanting to explore since he first learnt to walk.' Looking across to the man in uniform, he gave a nod. 'You can count me in, Bill.'

'And me,' said Ferris.

'Me too,' added Noel Oakley from his other side.

Similar offers quickly followed from just about every man in the room.

'How about you, Corey? I can provide you with a mount, or a bike, if you want one,' proffered someone from amongst the crowd.

'Thanks, Don, a horse will do fine,' Corey accepted amiably.

'And you, Kurt, are you coming too?' the man named Don now asked, watchfully.

The arch of Dale's brows rose slightly higher. So she wasn't the only one to have noticed Kurt's silence on the matter.

'I—er . . .' Kurt shifted uneasily on his stool and shook his blond head. 'No, I think I'll have to give it a miss this time, I'm sorry. We're—er—pretty busy at home at the moment, and since Karl's going . . .' His brother had already offered his services along with the others.

Don didn't comment—no one did—he just looked, hard-eyed and contemptuous, and Kurt rushed on in a defensively aggressive tone, 'In any case, I can't see why you need such a large ground party, anyway! With all the planes that are owned in the area, I'd have thought an aerial search would make more sense . . . as well as being a damned sight quicker.'

'Quicker at what? Getting rid of the planes and the pilots?' suggested Noel with unconcealed sarcasm.

'Mmm, with that many in the air and at the altitude they'd need to fly to spot a four-year-old, we'd probably have more downed planes and dead pilots than you could throw a stick at by the end of the day,' concurred another voice, and just as scornfully dismissing.

A mottled red stain showed beneath Kurt's tanned skin, but whether it had been caused by anger or chagrin, Dale couldn't tell. 'Well, I still don't see that it's . . .' he began.

'You're definitely not coming, then?' Don cut him off summarily.

Kurt's eyes chilled to a frosty hue. 'As I said . . .'

'Yeah, that's what I thought!' the slightly older man broke in again, disdainfully, and deliberately turning his back, finished the contents of the can he had been holding. 'Well, I guess I'd better be moving if I'm going to be at Andiah by sun-up. I'll see the rest of you in the morning,' he said to them generally as he began heading for the doorway—adding for Corey, in particular, with a grin. 'And I'll have that mount with me that I promised you, old son. You can depend on it.'

Corey acknowledged the remark with a raised can and a reciprocal grin, but Kurt watched the exchange with a resentful scowl.

'That smug bastard, Don Chatfield!' he snarled infuriatedly under his breath. 'Who does he think he is, turning his back on me like that? He and Corey always were as thick as thieves!'

Not quite certain just what connection one comment had with the other, Dale stared at him dubiously. 'Maybe you should have joined the search, after all,' she proposed quietly. 'I mean, I've no doubt they've all got plenty of work to do too, but they're willing to give up their time in order to look for a lost child, and surely that's more important.'

'Is it?' he countered derisively, glancing round the steadily emptying bar. Most of the others were starting to leave now so that they too could prepare for the morrow. 'I would have said it was more important for Peggy White to keep a sharper eye on her blasted kids' whereabouts, and if she didn't have quite so many of them, then perhaps she'd be able to!'

'She's only got three!' Dale felt bound to protest. He made it sound as if she had a dozen or so. 'Besides, even if she just had the one, you still couldn't expect her to keep track of him for every minute of every day at that age. You have to let them out of your sight sometimes.'

'That still doesn't make it my responsibility to go looking for them, though, does it?' he retorted with a sullen grimace.

'Well, yes, as a matter of fact, that's exactly what I thought it did, if only because of the unwritten law of the outback that says you help your neighbour if and whenever you can.' She shook her head incredulously. 'For heaven's sake, Kurt, there's a child lost out there somewhere! Who cares how or why he got there? The only thing that matters is that he's found as soon as possible.'

'One searcher more or less isn't going to make the slightest difference to the outcome.'

'I don't know about that. If everyone thought in the same vein, then . . .'

'Oh, for crying out loud, get off my back, will you!' he erupted in exasperated accents, slamming his can of drink down on the bar and jumping to his feet. 'I'm not going, and that's all there is to it!'

Before Dale could recover from her surprise at his outburst, Karl chose that moment to approach them.

'Sorry to bust up your Saturday evening, but since we both came in the same vehicle I guess we'd better make tracks shortly. I'd like to get some sleep before setting off in the early hours of the morning,' he smiled ruefully at his brother.

Kurt took a cursory look at the watch encircling his wrist, the corners of his mouth pulling down in a disgruntled manner. 'Be damned, I'm not leaving at this hour! I'm going to the movies.' And with a challenging glance thrown in Dale's direction he brushed roughly past his brother, striding for the hall. At the door he nearly collided with Corey and Bill Cooper who were also heading for the entry, but without a word to either of them he continued on his angry way.

'Well, he's in a nice mood, isn't he?' Karl half smiled drily.

'I'm afraid he seems to have taken exception to my saying I thought he should have joined the search party,' Dale relayed despondently.

His partial smile broadened into a decided grin. 'Probably because it reminds him too vividly of our first years at Tavener's Bridge.'

'Oh?' she frowned curiously.

'Mmm, I reckon Corey must have spent most of his time looking for us after we'd managed to lose ourselves in those days, and . . .' he leant forward conspiratorially, 'if you don't let on I said so, I can tell you things haven't changed all that much now. That's the real reason he won't join that party, you know!'

Shades of her Uncle Irwin! She wouldn't have believed it. 'You mean he's nervous he might make a fool of himself by displaying some incompetence?'

Karl nodded. 'Unfortunately, neither of us seems to be endowed with the slightest sense of direction once we leave the beaten track,' he admitted ruefully.

'But you're going to Andiah,' she pointed out.

'Ah, yes, but that's the difference between us, you see,' he shrugged. 'I don't mind admitting I'm no bushman, so I expect they'll give me something to do that won't necessitate me charging off into the scrub on my own. Kurt, on the other hand, refuses to admit anything of the kind because he hates to think of anyone being able to do something he can't.'

'He'd prefer everyone to believe he isn't interested in helping to find Mickey White rather than confess he lacks bushcraft?' Dale's brows peaked high in disbelief.

'Apparently,' Karl confirmed on an ironic note. 'Not that I suspect it does him much good, though.'

'Everyone knows, anyway?' she deduced, recalling her uncle's remarks.

'I've always figured it was more than likely.'

'And all because of a false sense of pride,' she sighed somewhat irritatedly.

'Yeah, well, he'll have to sort out that problem on his own,' Karl dismissed the matter unconcernedly. 'Right now I'm for home and a couple of hours sleep.'

'You're taking the car?' Dale questioned hurriedly before he could move away.

'Of course I'm taking the car,' he laughed. 'I sure wasn't planning on walking all the way to Tavener's Bridge.'

'But—but what about Kurt? How will he get home?'

'Beats me,' he owned indifferently. 'Although *he* could always try walking, I suppose.'

Dale couldn't make up her mind whether he was joking or not. 'You still can't just leave him here!' she protested.

'Why not?' Karl's brown eyes widened facetiously. 'He's done it to me before now, when he's had a . . .' He came to a rapid halt and then hunched one shoulder uncomfortably. 'Well, as I said, he's done it to me.'

'But it might be days before there's another vehicle going out to Tavener's Bridge!'

'Then perhaps he should have thought of that before suddenly deciding he had a hankering to go to the movies,' he returned in slightly more clipped accents. 'But he needn't think I'm hanging around waiting for him just because he's stormed off in a temper. It's about time someone made him face up to the consequences of his actions.'

Once Karl had left, Dale continued mulling over his comments regarding his brother for some time, seriously beginning to wonder now if she did, in fact, know Kurt as well as she had thought she did. Some totally unanticipated revelations had come to light that evening, one way or another, and Karl's last cryptic remark had her suspecting there were other matters also of which she was completely unaware as yet. Kurt had often implied that his easygoing younger brother always needed someone to make his decisions for him, but she couldn't honestly say that was exactly how it had appeared to her tonight.

'Dale! Could you spare us a minute, please, lass?'

The call came from the other end of the counter, putting a brake on her musings, and on looking up she found her uncle Lester talking with Corey and Bill Cooper near the doorway leading into the hall.

'Yes, of course,' she answered amiably, making towards them, but puzzling as to why her presence should be required all the same.

'Bill was just asking if you'd mind giving Peggy White a hand out at Andiah while the search is on,' her uncle enlightened her as soon as she reached them. 'You know, to help prepare the food and serve it to the men, that kind of thing. There'll be a few other women there, from neighbouring properties and so forth, but the more there are the easier it will be, naturally. What do you think of the idea? You don't have to go if you don't want to, mind you,' he added hastily, as if not wanting her to feel she was being forced into agreeing.

'No, really, I'd like to go,' she reassured him earnestly. 'Poor Peggy must have more than enough on her mind already, so I'd be only too pleased to help in any way possible.'

'Thank you, I'm sure your assistance will be appreciated,' Bill Cooper smiled gratefully. His eyes flicked back to the two men beside him. 'And now I suppose I'd best be making my way down the street to see who else I can get to join us.'

Dale's uncle cast a wry glance round the bar. 'Hmm, since you've almost cleared us out of customers for the evening, let's hope you can do the same for our opposition too,' he bantered.

'I'll certainly do my best, believe me!' Bill consoled him with a laugh as he departed.

Dale turned to her uncle, her lips curving humorously. 'Just one small question ... do you think the car's capable of making the trip out to Andiah?' The only vehicle her relatives possessed had been around for a good many years and wasn't exactly known for its reliability.

'Probably not,' Lester conceded ruefully. 'But since you'll be travelling with Corey in his Land Rover, it doesn't have to be, fortunately.'

'There's no point in taking more vehicles than necessary,' supplemented Corey. Distinctly coolly, Dale thought. Apart from those few moments earlier, he seemed to have been avoiding her company as much as she had his since the afternoon he had visited Tavener's Bridge, and was undoubtedly no more pleased with this unavoidable arrangement than she was.

'I see,' she acknowledged glumly. 'What time would you like me ready to leave, then?'

'Around two, I should think. It will take a few

hours to get there.'

'And—and supplies?' she stammered next. His perturbing presence still had the power to unnerve her. 'Are the Whites expected to provide them, or does everyone take their own?'

'No, Bill will arrange those with Wally Draper,' Lester cut in to advise. Wally owned the solitary general store in Karraparinka. 'All you need to take is a pair of willing hands.'

'Plus maybe your toothbrush and a change of clothes,' added Corey in a dampening voice.

The implication in his words had Dale's eyes darkening in dismay. 'You think there's a likelihood Mickey may not be found in one day?'

'It's always a possibility,' he confirmed with obvious reluctance, running a hand around the back of his neck. 'You'd be surprised just how far people *can* walk at times when they're lost.'

'But he's only four! Surely he couldn't have travelled all that great a distance.'

'Don't you believe it! he recommended with an ironic half laugh. 'If Arnold and his men couldn't find him this afternoon, then it's a fair guess he's already farther from the homestead than you'd imagine, and likely to go even farther if he's found water . . . which it's to be hoped he has.'

There were distressing connotations inherent in that remark too, and an apprehensive expression crossed her features. 'You don't paint a very comforting picture,' she reproached dolefully.

His lips tilted wryly, regretfully. 'I'm sorry, that wasn't my intention. I merely meant that you shouldn't expect instant success in these matters.'

With her attention involuntarily caught for the

moment by the fascinating curve of his mouth, it was only when Dale realised that both men were regarding her somewhat quizzically as a result of her preoccupation that she returned to her senses, flushing selfconsciously.

'No, I suppose not,' she immediately rushed to concur. And keeping her eyes determinedly fixed on her uncle this time, she continued in the same hasty vein, 'Well, if there's nothing else you wanted to see me about . . .'

'Mmm, you'd better be getting to bed if you're going to be doing the driving,' stated Corey calmly.

'I wasn't aware I was!' she exclaimed in surprise, and had no option but to look at him now. 'Am I?'

'Uh-huh,' he drawled lazily. 'Because that's when I plan to be doing my sleeping. Although, now I come to think of it,' he sent Lester a whimsical glance, 'perhaps I should have asked how she drives first.'

Dale gave a caustic grimace and answered for herself. 'With my hands on the wheel, the same as everyone else,' she quipped facetiously.

'And you're used to a four-wheel-drive, are you?' Corey's gold-flecked eyes held hers relentlessly.

'Well, I wouldn't say I was exactly—er—used to driving one,' she allowed nonchalantly.

'Neither would I!' her uncle burst out, laughing. 'As far as I know she's never even been in one, let alone driven one. At least, she hasn't since she's been in Karra.'

Dale wrinkled her nose at him in mock disgust. 'You didn't have to tell him that, though, did you?' Then, returning Corey's gaze indignantly, mimicked,

'Perhaps I should have asked how she drives first! You wouldn't have said that if it had been another man going with you, would you?'

'Probably not,' he admitted aggravatingly. 'But in your case it appears to have been justified, doesn't it?'

'*Touché*,' chuckled her uncle, and a grudging smile began edging the corners of her mouth upwards in response.

'Only because I haven't driven a four-wheel-drive, not because I can't drive at all,' was still as far as she was prepared to concede. 'Anyway,' she rallied, 'if Corey's so doubtful regarding my competence, why can't he have his sleep now like the rest of us?'

'Because there's equipment and supplies to be loaded and by the time everything's arranged, it probably wouldn't be worthwhile,' Corey answered for himself.

'But I thought you said Bill Cooper was attending to the supplies.' She spoke directly to him this time.

'Mmm, he's arranging them, but others will be doing the loading. That way we all get the chance of some sleep.'

Dale nodded her comprehension. 'Well, I guess I'll see you at two, then,' she said, starting to move away.

'Perhaps you'd better make that a quarter to two,' Corey suggested in a rather dry tone.

'Why's that?' she stopped to frown.

'Because even if you haven't the mechanics of my vehicle at heart, I have, and I'd like to know you're at least reasonably conversant with it before we set off,' he elucidated sardonically.

'I can hardly wait for the lessons to begin,' she mocked over one shoulder as she continued on through the doorway.

CHAPTER FOUR

'DALE! Are you there?'

Although muted, the call was still strong enough to penetrate Dale's sleep and she returned to consciousness with a guilty start, thinking she must have slept through the alarm of her bedside clock. It was pitch dark inside her room, but looking outwards she could just discern the outline of a man's figure in the space between the wide open french doors.

'I'm sorry,' she apologised breathlessly as she threw off her single covering sheet and set her feet to the floor. 'I'll be with you in a moment.'

'What are you doing in bed in the first place? I thought you said we'd be able to talk after the movies finished.'

'Kurt!' she gasped in surprise. In truth, she'd forgotten he was still in town.

In the dim light she could see him stiffen as she fumbled for and slipped into her housecoat. 'Who else were you expecting?' he queried sharply.

'No one,' she denied, combing her hair into place with her fingers and moving towards him. 'I just hadn't anticipated seeing you, that's all.'

'But you must have known I'd come back here after the movies.'

'Yes, well, with regard to that . . .'

'Look, I'm sorry for how I behaved earlier,' he broke in anxiously, catching hold of her shoulders to draw her nearer. 'I shouldn't have lost my temper with you,

it wasn't your fault.' He uttered a remorseful half
laugh. 'I guess I must have had more to drink than I
realised.'

Dale shrugged impassively. 'It doesn't matter. I
was . . .'

'You could have knocked me down with a feather,
though, when I asked Irwin where you were and he
said you'd gone to bed,' he cut her off again in his
desire to continue. 'I thought you must have been
really annoyed with me, but I'm relieved to see you're
not. I was imagining you and Karl tearing me to shreds
between you. Where is he, anyway? I couldn't see him
as your uncles were closing up the bar.'

Dale moved restively from one foot to the other. 'No,
he—er—he's probably back at Tavener's Bridge by
now, I expect,' she advised hesitantly.

'You mean, he took the car and left me stranded?'
Kurt's voice rose in wrathful disbelief.

'He said he . . .'

'The sneaky, rotten mongrel!' he interrupted yet
again to denounce lividly. 'Just wait until I get my
hands on him! I suppose he thought it was a huge joke
knowing the hell Black Jack'll give me when I do get
home.'

Something he apparently hadn't considered when
he'd done the same to his brother, she mused, but a
particular timbre in his voice had her disregarding
the thought and her head inclining curiously.

'Is your stepfather really as hard as everyone says he
is, Kurt?' She had only met the man twice, and then
only so briefly that she hadn't been able to form any
sort of an opinion for herself, except to note that he
was very tall and solidly built, and a strikingly handsome man for his age.

'Is he ever!' His expressive exclamation wasn't meant to leave any doubts in her mind. 'There aren't many who don't quake when Jack Tavener roars, believe me!' With a reminiscent laugh that had something akin to a nervous catch in it.

'Including Corey?' she just had to probe, even if tentatively.

'Oh, no, not Corey,' he partly heaved, partly snorted sardonically. 'Why would he? They're two of a kind, and he can be as ruthless and unyielding as his old man when he wants to be! For the last couple of years before he left home it used to be a real clash of the titans, I can tell you. Neither of them would give way to the other, although I must admit there were times when I suspected they enjoyed the baiting that went on. Nonetheless, about the only thing I ever knew them to instantly agree on was the way in which the property should be run. Still, at least it did Karl and me a favour. It kept Black Jack so occupied he didn't have time to be taking us to task as well,' he recalled on a thankful note.

'It must also have been very hard on your mother, trying to keep the peace,' she surmised contemplatively.

'Not really.' She felt rather than saw him shrug unconcernedly in the darkness. 'As long as Karl and I weren't involved, I don't think it worried her greatly. Blood's certainly thicker than water where she's concerned, and always will be. I mean, let's face it, as everyone knew, it was no love match when she married Jack Tavener. It was purely a marriage of convenience on both sides, so why should she worry herself with what happened between Corey and his father?'

And especially not when her strongest wish was,

apparently, to obtain Tavener's Bridge for her own two sons! added Dale silently, astringently.

'Anyhow, I didn't come here to discuss family matters,' Kurt went on with careless indifference. 'Although, now I come to think of it, perhaps one member of it has done me a favour, after all.'

'How do you mean?' Dale reluctantly brought her attention back to what he was saying.

'Well, Karl's having stranded me here isn't without its benefits, is it?' he enlightened her with sudden good humour. 'It means that until someone either comes in from the property, or there's someone going out that way, I can spend all my time with you.'

Dale shifted uneasily again. 'Except that I'm going out to Andiah in a few hours' time,' she told him in an apologetic voice.

Kurt's hands abruptly dropped from her shoulders and in the silence of the night his harshly indrawn breath was very audible. 'Why?' he demanded, his mood altering rapidly. 'Because you want to appear as noble-minded as the rest of them? Or could it perhaps just have something to do with the fact that Corey's going?'

'Neither, actually,' she replied a little coolly, not liking either of his rather snidely stressed inferences. 'I'm going because Bill Cooper asked me if I'd give Peggy White a hand, and that's also the reason I went to bed early. We're planning on leaving at two.'

'We?' he immediately questioned.

Her chin lifted defiantly. 'That's right. As it so happens I'm going with Corey in his Land Rover.'

'And who arranged that, I wonder?'

'Well, it wasn't me, if that's what you're thinking! I believe it may have been Uncle Les, if you really want to know. I was just presented with a *fait accompli*.'

Kurt sighed remorsefully and brushed the fingers of one hand lightly down the side of her face from cheek to chin. 'I'm sorry, I guess I must just be in a suspicious mood tonight. Forgive me?'

'Only if you stop accusing me of being interested in Corey every time I mention his name,' she stipulated wryly. She could be interested in the circumstances surrounding the man, without being interested in the man himself, couldn't she? 'I'm travelling with him out of necessity, not because I wanted it that way, I can assure you.'

'But why travel with him at all? Why not say you've changed your mind about going and stay here in Karra with me?' he proposed eagerly.

'I couldn't do that!' she gasped, sounding somewhat more shocked than regretful. 'They're expecting me to help now, and I wouldn't like to go back on my word. How about you change *your* mind instead and come with us? It would be better than sitting around town doing nothing, surely?'

He seemed to take offence at that, for he promptly retorted, 'Who said I intended doing nothing? If you're so obviously uninterested in keeping me company, then just maybe I'll find someone else who is!'

A week ago his threat might have caused her some slight apprehension but, surprisingly, it didn't now. 'That's up to you, of course,' she allowed stiffly.

'Because you just don't care, do you?'

'I don't care for being threatened, if that's what you mean.'

'Oh, hell!' Kurt ran a hand distractedly through his blond hair. 'I didn't really intend it as a threat, Dale. It was more of a misguided attempt to make you jealous, because I want you here with me.' He caught her to him possessively. 'You must know by now how serious my feelings are where you're concerned. It's you I want, honey, no one else. I just wish I could believe you felt the same way about me.'

'Oh, Kurt,' she murmured helplessly. 'Of course I like you. It—it's just that I still feel I haven't known you all that long, and . . .' She faltered to a halt, turning an entreating face up to his. 'Please don't rush me.'

His hold tightened convulsively, his mouth finding hers unerringly even in the dark, but no sooner had Dale begun to respond than she discovered, to her alarmed dismay, that she was measuring his caresses—unfavourably—against those of his stepbrother, and she pulled herself free in mortification.

'I'm sorry, I must be on edge wondering whether they'll manage to find little Mickey White tomorrow, I guess,' she apologised lamely on feeling him tense as a result of her rejection.

'Then if it's worrying you to that degree, maybe you shouldn't go at all.' Relaxing, Kurt bent his head close again, his breath warm against her lips when he spoke. 'Perhaps you should stay in Karra with me. If you'll just let me, I'll take your mind off what's happening at Andiah,' he promised thickly.

'Mmm, possibly you could, but I don't think I'd better let you try all the same,' she half laughed shakily, gently but purposefully disentangling herself from exploring hands that were becoming as explicitly insistent as his words. 'In fact, as I'm to be doing the driving when we leave, I think it might be best if you allowed me to get some more sleep, while you see Uncle Les or Uncle Irwin about somewhere to bed down yourself before they close up completely for the night and you miss out altogether.'

'If I did, you'd let me share with you, wouldn't you?' he cajoled hopefully, reaching for her once more.

'Uh-uh, sorry,' she refused in an ironic tone as she carefully evaded his grasp. 'And now I really will have to ask you to leave, please, Kurt.'

He didn't appear to have heard her as he pressed persuasively, 'Not even for a couple of hours?'

She shook her head decisively. 'Not even for a couple of minutes.'

'You really mean to go to Andiah, then?' he sighed.

'Yes, I do,' she nodded, and raising herself up on her toes placed a light, brief kiss on his lips. 'But I'll see you when I get back, okay?'

'I suppose so,' he conceded with a fatalistic hunching of his shoulders. 'If you won't stay, I don't seem to have much choice in the matter, do I?'

Now it was Dale's turn to shrug, ruefully. 'As I said, you could always come with us.'

'No, thanks,' he squashed that idea very swiftly. 'You already know my feelings in that regard.'

'In that case . . .' She held her hands expressively wide.

'Yeah, I know . . . there's nothing more to be said,' he both drawled and grimaced at the same time as he thrust his hands into the back pockets of his pants and started to turn away. 'So I guess I'll see you later.'

With a mute nod, Dale watched him make his way along the verandah to the doors leading into the hall and then returned to her bed.

It seemed hardly any time later that the shrill ringing of her alarm clock had her awake again, and with a barely suppressed groan she groped frantically for the switch to turn it off before its cacophonous pealing wakened everyone else in the hotel as well.

Breathing a sigh of relief for the peace that followed, she hurriedly washed and dressed, then with her previously packed overnight bag in her hand tiptoed over the old, creaking floorboards and out into the street. The Land Rover was parked immediately in front of the hotel, although Corey was nowhere to be seen, and walking across to it Dale tossed her bag in its loaded rear and then climbed into the driver's seat in order to familiarise herself with the controls while she awaited his return.

'All set?'

The deeply toned query as he slid on to the seat beside her a few minutes later and slammed the door closed after him had Dale pulling a wry face. 'For my first lesson, you mean?'

'Oh, that's right. I'd forgotten,' he grinned so lazily as he tipped his wide brimmed bush hat farther back on his head that Dale felt her stomach somersault wildly. 'Well, let's get to it, then.'

Shortly, his explanations completed, her lips began curving ruefully. 'In other words, for the type of driving I'll be doing, it's hardly any different from a conventional car!'

'Mmm, I guess you could say that,' he affirmed nonchalantly.

'And to find that out I needed to get up a quarter of an hour earlier?' Her brows rose caustically high.

'How was I to know you'd realise the similarities so quickly?' he countered in an innocent tone.

Dale slanted him a sideways glance that spoke volumes. 'You know, one could easily reach the stage of wanting to slap you, Corey Tavener,' she advised drily. 'Last night you deliberately set out to make driving this thing sound far more difficult than it really is, didn't you?'

His eyes shone with impenitent laughter. 'It seemed reasonable at the time,' he owned, flexing broad shoulders.

'Heel!' she denounced with a reluctant half laugh. 'Somehow I think I'm better off when you're not talking to me.'

'As you please, angel,' he drawled compliantly, wedging himself comfortably between the seat and the door, and tipping his hat down over his eyes this time. 'I won't say another word till we arrive.'

Dale's lips quirked eloquently. 'Yes, well, although that's extremely obliging of you, before you nod off to sleep it still might be an idea if you told me just how I get to Andiah, don't you think? I know it's out there somewhere,' waving a hand in the general direction, 'but as to which particular road I'm supposed to take, I'm afraid I haven't a clue.'

'Just follow Bill and he'll lead you straight there,' Corey directed without moving on hearing the sound of an approaching vehicle. 'But don't get too close or we'll fill up with dust once we leave town.'

With a wry smile of understanding, Dale switched the engine into life and began following the police wagon down the street. 'I thought there'd be more than just those two vehicles leaving from Karra,' she commented in surprise.

'Mmm, so there were, but most of them have gone already.' Folding his arms across his chest, he settled himself further down in the seat. 'The rest are due to follow shortly.'

'Then, judging by the response in the pub, there should be quite a number of people out there, shouldn't there?' she went on speculatively.

'More than likely.'

Which, of course, would mean the chances of finding Mickey would be greater, she surmised hopefully. 'Do you want me to wake you up as soon as we reach Andiah, or wait until we arrive at the homestead?'

'Considering you haven't stopped talking since we started to move, I'm beginning to suspect neither will be necessary,' he returned on a sardonic note.

'Oh!' She chewed at her lip disconcertedly. 'I'm sorry, it's just that I've never been connected with anything like this before.'

'So I gathered.' His answer was mockingly given.

Wrinkling her nose at the windscreen, Dale determined not to say another word, but as her thoughts strayed so often and so waywardly to matters concerning him, it was an impossible resolve to keep, and after a few kilometres she couldn't help but break it altogether.

'Corey?' she murmured cautiously.

'Mmm?'

'Where do you live these days?'

'Denham,' came the reply in the same languid tone, and which had her mouth shaping into a reminiscent smile. When he was half asleep his voice had a warm, rich quality to it like deep velvet.

'Where's that?' she asked next, unable to place the name.

'South-west.'

'Queensland?'

'Uh-huh,' he nodded almost imperceptibly.

Although she felt mean not letting him go to sleep, while he was in such a drowsy state did appear to be the only times she could extract any information from him, and she pressed on regardless.

'Have you lived there ever since you left Karraparinka?'

'No.' Accompanied by a very brief shake of his head on this occasion.

And not terribly enlightening, Dale had to admit. 'How long have you been there, then?' she ventured to probe a little further.

'Long enough ... and that applies to your question time too,' he returned in somewhat less leisurely accents. Lifting his hat slightly, he sent her a lazily assessing glance from beneath its brim. 'You do have a penchant for seeking answers when a man's least prepared, don't you, angel?'

Dale hastily swung her gaze back to the front. 'I'm sorry, I was just making conversation,' she burst out protectively.

'With someone who's trying to sleep?'

The touch of amusement laced with mockery in his voice had her cheeks burning feverishly. Why, in heaven's name, hadn't she learnt from her past mistakes!

'I—I—it was lonely with no one to talk to,' she stammered feebly.

'Already?' There was far more than just a hint of amusement evident now. 'We've only been on the road for ten minutes. How are you going to be after a couple of hours?'

Fortunately, however, his increasingly taunting tone was just the spur Dale needed to regain her composure, at least in part, and drawing a quick breath to calm her inner turmoil, she assumed as insouciant a pose as possible.

'Quite used to it by then, I expect,' she predicted

airily. 'So please go back to sleep. I'm sorry I woke you. It won't happen again, I promise.' Nothing was more certain!

To her relief, Corey seemed inclined to comply with her suggestion as he dropped his hat back into its previously covering position, then promptly shattered the illusion by drawling, 'And as I recall, I recommended you ask Kurt for any information you wanted in future.'

As she remembered it, he hadn't so much recommended as ordered! 'So you did,' she grimaced. 'But if I had asked him instead, would he have known where you live now?'

'I doubt it,' he owned drily. 'But then I suspect Kurt isn't so much interested in where I've been for the last eight years as he is in where I'm likely to be for the next eight.'

Although Dale knew immediately just what he was meaning, two completely differing emotions prevented her from going to Kurt's defence as she first intended. One was surprise due to Corey's having made such a comment without any prompting—and especially when only moments before he had reminded her once again that he preferred to keep his affairs private—while the other was wariness, because she was unsure whether she should even admit to knowing what he was talking about.

When she didn't reply, Corey lifted his hat slightly again and cast her a mocking glance. 'Well?' he prompted laconically.

'I don't know what you mean,' she finally parried weakly.

'Don't know . . . or won't admit?'

The shrewd gibe had her forgetting all about caution

as her chin angled resentfully. 'As far as I know, there's nothing to admit! At least, not where Kurt's concerned,' honesty forced her to amend.

'And Louise . . . who calls the tune he jumps to?'

Dale stared at him incredulously for so long that she almost ran them off the road. 'Oh, she does not!' she denied scornfully after swerving back on to the track. 'Kurt makes his own decisions.'

'If you say so,' he acquiesced wryly, unexpectedly, with a shrug.

But the fact that he did give in so easily made it appear he was humouring her and, in consequence, her prior confidence diminished considerably. 'Well, doesn't he?'

'Not unless he's altered a good deal, and from what I hear, that doesn't seem to be the case.'

Dale chewed at her lower lip musingly. Could that, perhaps, have been the reason for Kurt's change of attitude from mild disconcertment to moody resentment regarding his stepbrother's return, then? Because his mother had been to work on him in the meantime? It was feasible when she knew of nothing else that could have generated such a fractious reversal.

'Disquieting, hmm?' Corey speculated indolently.

Actually, it was a little, she had to confess—even if only to herself—but at the same time she was experiencing a strange sense of foreboding that there was still more to it than met the eye.

'Why are you suddenly telling me all this?' she frowned as she flicked him a quizzical glance.

His firm, sensuous mouth curved crookedly. 'Maybe to gauge your reaction.'

'For what purpose?' The puzzled creases which had

formed between her brows now disappeared as her brows peaked in astonishment.

Corey stretched his long legs calmly, and yet she suspected he was nowhere near as relaxed as he looked. 'W-e-ll,' he drew the word out softly, 'you do ask an inordinate amount of questions, don't you, my sweet? And since you and Kurt are—er—more than just mere acquaintances, then I guess it could be said you also have something of a vested interest in what happens at Tavener's Bridge, couldn't it?'

Indignation swept through Dale like a raging inferno and she brought the Land Rover to a skidding halt in order to give vent to it without any distractions.

'You think I'm pumping you for information just so I can pass it on to Kurt, is that what you're trying to say?' she rounded on him fiercely. 'Well, how dare you! As if I would! I told you Kurt doesn't own me, and you've no right to accuse me of something so—so sly and underhanded! The only reason I asked those questions was because—was because . . .'

'Mmm?' he inserted in a bantering tone, and looking so at ease once more that she could only presume her reaction had passed muster. Not that that gave her any satisfaction, however.

'Oh, go to sleep, Corey!' she flared. 'I'd hate you to fall off your horse later today because you were too tired to stay awake!' Shades of sarcasm began creeping into her voice.

He tut-tuttered mockingly, but lowered his hat over his eyes again. 'I'm yours to command, angel.'

With a smouldering glare, Dale resumed driving. So he was hers to command, was he? she grimaced acidly. That would be the day! She doubted there was a woman alive who could ever command the aggravating, ultra-masculine Corey Tavener!

'And I'm not "angel", or "your sweet" either!' she muttered rebelliously to herself in the same caustic vein.

Corey's lips might have twitched imperceptibly, but there was no comment forthcoming, and they continued along the road in silence.

CHAPTER FIVE

THE first pale streaks of morning light were just beginning to appear on the horizon when Dale and Corey arrived at Andiah homestead, and from the number of vehicles already present it soon became obvious that almost every able-bodied man in the district had heeded the Whites' call for assistance.

That was, almost every man except Kurt, Dale couldn't help remembering disappointedly, and even a trifle embarrassedly on his behalf since he had shown himself to be so uncaring. If he wouldn't even put a lost child before his own ego, then maybe it wasn't surprising the rest of the community treated him with a certain amount of reserve. Or was it contempt? The insidious thought followed unbidden, but she flinched away from it, discomfited, lest it force her to analyse her own thoughts on the matter more deeply.

'We're here.' She leant across to shake Corey awake after parking between a truck and a station wagon, and nearly jumped out of her skin when her hand was suddenly arrested in mid-air.

'Good grief! What on earth made you do that?' she exclaimed shakily, looking down at the strong, tanned fingers which hadn't yet released hers. 'You frightened me out of my wits! I thought you were still asleep.'

'Sorry,' he grinned wryly, settling his hat into a conventional position as he eased himself upright. 'But after your comment last night, I figured it was better to be safe than sorry.'

Momentarily, she stared at him in bewilderment. Then her violet eyes began to sparkle with realisation and she gave a rueful, grudging laugh. 'Don't worry, I wouldn't have waited this long if I was intending to deal out some physical retribution. I would have done it hours ago . . . when the mood was really upon me.'

'So what stopped you?'

'Oh, I don't know,' she shrugged selfconsciously, becoming increasingly aware of the warmth of his hand which continued to hold hers. 'Probably the fact that I've always thought it was unfair to take advantage of the knowledge that a man can't—or, at least, isn't supposed to,' she corrected with a shy half smile, 'hit back.'

'You sound just like my mother,' he commented humorously. 'She was always strong on what was fair and what wasn't.'

'Your real mother, you mean?' tentatively.

Releasing her at last, Corey clasped his hands behind his head, stretching. 'Uh-huh.'

'You were only twelve when she died, weren't you?' she went on cautiously. It was the first time he had ever mentioned his mother.

'Something like that,' he concurred.

'I expect you must have missed her very much at that age.' The more so with his father apparently blaming him for her death.

Corey exhaled heavily, his lips twisting wryly. 'Everybody did,' he divulged finally. 'She was one of those people who somehow manage to make the world seem a nicer place to live in. What with her tremendous sense of fun and unbounded zest for life, she . . .'

'Yes?' Dale waited expectantly.

Even white teeth showed in a beguiling, lopsided

smile that caught and held her gaze hypnotically. 'I should have known, shouldn't I?' He shook his head ruefully. 'It's getting to be a habit talking to you when I'm off guard . . . and then saying more than I intend.'

'Because you still don't trust me?' Her eyes became tinged with despondency.

Opening the door on his side, he partly turned towards it. 'It's not so much you I don't trust, angel, as myself,' he advised ironically over his shoulder.

'Because you're frightened you might accidentally let someone know what you're thinking?' she charged recklessly.

Corey finished alighting, then looked back into the interior of the vehicle, his expression one of warning laced with mockery. 'When you can give me a satisfactory reason as to why I should confide in you, in particular, then I'll give you an answer to that.'

Dale looked away from his gold-flecked eyes disconcertedly. Why should he tell her any of his thoughts? She meant nothing to him. 'I'm sorry,' she offered faintly.

'So you keep saying.'

The satirical dryness in his tone had her bristling resentfully. 'Then I'll make it a point not to do so again!' she snapped. 'Does that suit you better?'

Whether it did or not, she didn't discover, for a young woman in her early thirties with light brown hair and pale blue, vaguely protruding eyes, suddenly swept down on them from the direction of the homestead.

'Corey! Corey darling!' she cooed affectionately. Or was it affectedly? grimaced Dale with unusual acrimony as she stepped down to the ground. 'We heard you were back and I was hoping to see you here today,' the other woman continued in the same gushing voice. 'But who's this you've brought with you? Don't tell me you're married!' sounding almost alarmed as she subjected Dale to a hard, penetrating scrutiny.

Ignoring the embarrassed warmth which spread into her cheeks, Dale forced herself to return the woman's stare as coolly as it had been given, and leaving Corey to disclaim with an unconcerned laugh, 'No, I still haven't surrendered my freedom. Dale is Les and Irwin's niece. Bill Cooper asked if she'd mind lending you ladies a hand.' His brows rose enquiringly. 'Haven't you two met before?'

Dale merely shook her head, but the older girl obviously felt the matter required further comment. 'Hardly!' she laughed on a somewhat scoffing note. 'You know I never go into Karraparinka unless it's absolutely unavoidable, and as for patronising any of the hotels . . . well, I've always considered that best left to the men. Naturally, I've heard talk of the Freeman brothers' niece, though. You're Kurt Agnew's latest little friend, aren't you?' she smiled condescendingly at Dale.

'I guess you could say that,' Dale allowed with an indifferent shrug. 'Although it would appear you have the advantage of me, *Mrs . . .*?' She stressed explicitly on noting the other woman's glittering wedding rings.

'Bryson . . . Opal Bryson. And even though we've never met before, I expect you've heard of me, anyway, haven't you?' came the smug reply.

'No, I can't say I have, now that you mention it,' Dale didn't mind informing her sweetly. That kind of insufferable self-satisfaction just seemed to invite retaliation! 'Although I'm glad to have made your acquaintance, Mrs Bryson. I mainly get to meet the younger members of the community at the pub, so it's nice to meet some of the *old* residents too.'

As the pale blue eyes of the woman beside him became decidedly protruding, with anger, Corey's thickly lashed eyes narrowed. 'I think you can safely call Opal by her first name, Dale,' he advised wryly. 'There's no need to show quite that much respect, since at thirty-two, I don't consider either of us to be in our dotage just yet.'

With a defiant lift of her chin—she wasn't too happy with him at the moment either!—Dale assumed a limpid expression. 'Oh, I do apologise!' she exclaimed with feigned regret. 'I only meant to be polite, not to imply that Opal was over the hill! Of course, it's different for a man. He's considered to be in his prime in his thirties, whereas a woman . . .!' She clapped a hand over her mouth in artless dismay. 'Oh, dear, there I go again! I suppose I'll just have to ask you to make allowances for the thoughtlessness of youth, but I expect you can still remember what it was like to be my age, can't you?'

'Only with some considerable effort, of course,' retorted Corey sarcastically.

'Personally, I wouldn't want to remember!' claimed Opal with icy hauteur. 'I couldn't imagine anything worse than being at such an insensitive, gauche, and insecure age again.'

Dale's lips pursed ruefully. Were those descriptions recollections from Opal's past, or evaluations of herself? She deduced it was most probably the latter.

'Yes, well, if you'll excuse me, this insensitive, gauche, and insecure child will go and say a few words to Peggy,' she smiled facetiously, and promptly set off for the homestead. As far as she was concerned, a respite from both of them would be welcome!

There were groups of people clustered everywhere around and in front of the house, and passing between a row of stationary vehicles, Dale headed for those nearest. Before she could reach them, however, a forceful hand descended on to her shoulder from behind and brought her to a halt.

'Just what the hell's got into you, hmm?' demanded Corey peremptorily.

To Dale's surprise Opal wasn't still with him, but even if she had been it was doubtful whether her response would have been any more co-operative.

'I don't know what you're talking about,' she denied, shrugging away from his touch.

'Not much you don't! Your behaviour back there was outrageous!'

'Mine was?' she exploded indignantly. 'What about hers? Or am I supposed to just humbly accept her patronising remarks because she apparently considers herself a cut above everyone else?' Her eyes widened tartly.

'Oh, stop making mountains out of molehills!' He shook his head exasperatedly. 'That's merely her way of talking. She's always been like it.'

'Well, bully for her! In that case, maybe I'll just have to change *my* way in future too! Although I can understand why you find her attitude acceptable, of course. I mean, she was hoping "*Corey darling*" would be here today, wasn't she?' she copied with biting mockery.

'So?' One amused brow flicked upwards.

Dale stared at him fixedly, her thoughts whirling as if caught in a storm. So she was jealous, she abruptly realised in tormenting despair. Resentfully, agonisingly, and unbelievably jealous of Opal's openly proprietorial air towards him. Her gaze wavered treacherously and she half turned away.

'So why don't you just leave me alone!' she ordered on a fretful note. 'Just because I drove over with you it doesn't mean I'm in your charge, or that you can read me the riot act whenever you feel like it!'

'Not even if it's warranted?'

'That's only your opinion, not mine,' she returned his wry humour with morose defiance.

'Mmm, I know. That's what makes it so curious.' Catching her by the nape of her neck, he determinedly tipped her face up to his, drawling reflectively, 'You're not acting at all like your usual self, angel.'

She didn't need him to tell her that! Although why she should have been jealous of Opal, she didn't really know. She was quite content dating Kurt, wasn't she? With an irritable movement she forced her thoughts back into line.

'Because I took exception to her smug comments?' she queried with a grimace.

'Because of the manner in which you showed your annoyance,' he elucidated drily. 'You were a malicious little cat!'

'So was she!' Dale retorted excusingly, uncomfortably, knowing he was right. 'But I bet you didn't censure her for it, Oh no, as I recall, you made excuses for her, didn't you?

'No, I didn't make excuses for her,' he denied, giving her an annoyed shake. 'I merely stated the facts . . . in an effort to make you realise there was no need for you to copy her because Opal, unfortunately, reacts that way to most other members of her own sex.' His head lowered, and he continued in a softer tone, 'Whereas you, my sweet, I suspect, do not.'

'Oh!' Feeling foolishly pleased at his supposition, Dale averted her gaze swiftly lest her eyes revealed her unreasonable satisfaction. 'Well, I wasn't to know that was the reason, was I?' she shrugged defensively.

'And now that you do?'

'I—I'll keep it in mind, I guess,' was as far as she was prepared to concede. She didn't want him thinking she was ready to fall in with his every wish just because he'd implied she had a nicer disposition than Opal.

Corey's lips twisted sardonically. 'Your tractability positively takes my breath away,' he mocked.

'I'm so glad,' she smiled, equally taunting, and deliberately misconstruing his meaning. 'I wouldn't have wanted you to think I was unappreciative.'

'Nor I of you, you provoking little jade!' he drawled as his hand slid upwards to tangle within her hair, immobilising her head while his mouth took possession of hers with an insistence that snatched both her own breath as well as her flippancy away.

'Corey . . . stop it!' she gasped frantically as soon as she was able. 'Everyone can see us!'

'Only if they happen to be looking,' he murmured with dismaying unconcern before resuming his devastating exploration of her ungovernably responsive lips.

Not wanting to attract undue attention by struggling too violently—just in case they weren't already being observed—Dale had no option but to confine herself to ineffectual attempts at either pushing or pulling herself free, while at the same time trying desperately to regain control of the traitorous emotions which had flared into unruly life at the touch of his firm mouth.

'Will you stop doing that!' she instructed raggedly, vexedly, the minute he raised his head a second time.

'All right, so maybe I shouldn't have said what I did, but you've had your revenge now, and what if Kurt should hear about this?'

Although his grip had relaxed, it hadn't been removed, and amber eyes surveyed her still upturned face leisurely. 'I thought you said he didn't own you,' he reminded her softly.

'But neither do you, Corey!' she impressed on him hastily. 'And—and oh, God, here comes Karl and your friend Don Chatfield!' On a stricken note, seeing the two men approaching, 'Please let go of me now!'

'Saved in the nick of time, huh?' he grinned wryly, but to her relief finally consenting to release her. 'And just when things were beginning to get interesting too.'

'That's a matter of opinion!' she muttered acidly out of the corner of her mouth, then smiled at the other two men as they reached them. 'Good morning!' And to Karl, 'Did you manage to get some sleep, after all?'

'Some being the operative word,' he agreed with graphic feeling. 'A couple of times I thought I was going to doze off at the wheel on the way here.'

'Well, at least you came,' put in Don heavily. 'That's more than can be said for some.'

No one needed to ask just who he meant hadn't put in an appearance, and it was Dale who rushed into speech in order to break the rather taut silence that followed.

'Just how many would you say are here? There seems a tremendous amount,' she marvelled as a number of planes now began joining the vehicles that were still arriving.

Don scanned the area cursorily. 'Oh, upwards of two hundred, I should imagine. Perhaps close to three.'

By common consent they started moving towards the

homestead. 'With that many you shouldn't have too much trouble finding him, should you?' Dale proposed in hopeful tones.

'I don't know about that, but we'll certainly give it a bloody good try,' he half laughed ruefully. 'Because it won't be pleasant for the little feller out there today. All the signs point to it being a real scorcher.'

Until that moment Dale hadn't really noticed just how warm it was for that hour of the day, but now that her attention had been drawn to it she realised there had been very little breeze during the night to relieve the previous day's heat, which meant that the temperature would climb even more rapidly than usual once the sun cleared the tree-tops.

'Poor Mickey,' she frowned sympathetically. 'Although I don't suppose the conditions will be too pleasant for the searchers either, will they?'

'Mmm, but then we're used to being out in it all day . . . he isn't.'

A thought-producing remark which had them continuing in temporary silence.

Outside the homestead controlled disorder reigned as Bill Cooper busily organised separate parties to cover particular areas, maps were passed back and forth, equipment checked, mounts saddled, and last cups of tea taken from a trio of four-and-a-half-litre enamelled pots which, along with a wide assortment of mugs, had been deposited on a long trestle table on the verandah.

At the steps, Dale turned to her three companions with a smile. 'Well, if I don't happen to see you again before you leave, I wish you good luck and successful hunting.'

With reciprocal smiles, Karl and Don touched acknowledging fingers to the brims of their hats before heading towards Bill, but Corey didn't immediately follow them.

'You'll be okay on your own?' he stayed to query considerately. 'Or would you prefer an introduction to a few more of the ladies present?'

'No, I'll be all right. I think I already know most of them from their trips to town—but thank you just the same,' she replied shyly, both surprised and touched by his unexpected solicitude. Somehow, she doubted if it would have occurred to Kurt.

His head inclined indolently. 'My pleasure, angel. You just watch yourself, hmm?'

'Shouldn't I be saying that to you?' she countered with a shaky laugh. When they contained such a warm teasing light, those ebony-framed eyes of his made her feel as if she was wilting at the knees.

'Except I was under the impression you'd prefer it if I just exchanged places with young Mickey,' he drawled.

Glancing out at the hard beauty of the sere and searing Mitchell grass plains where dusty-leaved trees stood parched as they awaited the onset of the annual life-giving wet season, Dale shook her head faintly.

'I wouldn't wish it on anyone to be lost out there,' she half smiled.

From behind him someone called Corey's name and he raised a hand in response, although his sobering gaze didn't waver from the pensive face before him. 'You have a soft heart, Dale Freeman. For God's sake don't waste it on someone who'll mistrust it,' he urged in a suddenly deep voice. Then, in a return to his previous blithe mood, he grinned and flicked a finger towards the end of her nose as he took his leave with a brief, 'I'll see you later.'

Dale watched his loose-limbed progress across to the group clustered around Bill with puzzled lines scoring her smooth forehead. Had he been trying to warn her against becoming too involved with Kurt? And if so, why? Because, even though she had denied it, he believed Kurt meant more to her than he actually did, or—she experienced a sinking feeling in the pit of her stomach—because he was using her for some nefarious plan of his own? After all, from some of the remarks and comments that had been made so far it was obvious all wasn't quite as it should be between the two step-brothers, for one reason or another.

And if she did stop seeing Kurt, what then? Did Corey think that just because she had foolishly re-sponded to his kisses she was willing to fall into his arms like a ripe plum . . . just as Wanda Gilchrist had? she relentlessly forced herself to make the comparison. Rather than only seeing the physically attractive side of Corey Tavener, perhaps she should be concentrating on his unattractive reputation instead. It contained a warning she would do well to remember! A moment later, with that thought firmly fixed in her mind, she turned and entered the homestead.

Most of the women were in the kitchen, sorting out the food that Karl and a couple of other men were beginning to unload from the various vehicles used to transport it, and exchanging greetings with those she knew, Dale squeezed through to where Peggy White was refilling one of the large teapots.

'Dale! How nice of you to have come,' Peggy ex-claimed with genuine pleasure on seeing her.

'I was only too pleased to,' Dale replied, her gaze sympathetic. 'I just wish it could have been under happier circumstances, that's all.'

Momentarily, Peggy's expression faltered, then with a quick press of her lips she determinedly smiled again. 'Yes, well, young Mick's always been something of an explorer, I'm afraid, although he's never gone this far from home before. But they'll find him, I'm sure of that,' she nodded confidently in an evident attempt to convince herself, if no one else.

'Yes, of course they will,' Dale added her own reassurance. 'There's some very determined men outside.'

'Mmm, I know, and Arnold and I were so grateful to see them all arriving.'

'I can imagine,' smiled Dale understandingly. But on seeing Peggy's blue eyes becoming noticeably misty, she judiciously decided to change the subject by indicating the pot on the table and bantering, 'And quite a few of whom are probably waiting for this! Would you like me to take it out to them for you?'

'If you wouldn't mind.'

'While you're out there you may as well collect all the used mugs so they can be washed,' suggested Opal, apparently overhearing, and from the manner in which she had been giving Karl and the other men orders, obviously having designated herself as supervisor of the kitchen detail. 'That is, if you have no objection to being assigned to the washing up, of course.'

'No, I have no objection,' Dale shook her head impassively. If Opal had hoped to get an argument from her because of being given the most menial post to fulfil then the woman was doomed to disappointment. She had said she was willing to help in any way she could, and she'd meant it.

The sun was just beginning to make its appearance

on the horizon when Dale deposited the teapot on the table outside, and she knew it wouldn't be long now before the search got under way. In fact, some of the men were already mounted, but although her eyes waywardly sought Corey's commanding figure, she couldn't distinguish him among those immediately in front of the verandah and, stacking as many mugs as possible on the tray she had brought out with her, she reluctantly returned inside.

Half an hour later, Karl and the two men who had been helping him were the only males remaining at the homestead—it being their task to man a base communication station and to relay any necessary messages—and as the sound of the searchers' calling voices and cracking stockwhips faded in the distance, a feeling of nervous but hopeful expectancy settled over those left behind as they returned to what they had been doing.

'You can start slicing and buttering the bread, Margaret,' directed Opal, and making Dale smile wryly as she turned to the middle-aged woman who was drying the mugs for her after she washed them.

'Does Opal always do the organising at these sort of affairs?' she couldn't help asking.

'Mostly. At least whenever she's up here,' Alma Fletcher confirmed humorously.

'Doesn't anyone mind?'

'Not really,' Alma shrugged, and then uttered a soft, rueful laugh. 'You see, as Opal herself is only too willing to tell you, she's never had to wash a plate or actually prepare a meal in her life. She's always had others to do that for her. But . . .' she paused significantly, 'to give her her due, she is an excellent organiser, so in order to keep the peace—we suspect she'd have a convulsion if someone suggested she actually do some of the work—and since there's usually a crowd to lighten the load in any case, we just allow her to take charge on those occasions when she turns up. It saves one of us doing it, and she really isn't here all that often. Opal prefers to spend as much of her time as possible either at her apartment on the Gold Coast or jet-setting. She only returns to the Gulf to see her parents and her children occasionally.'

'They don't live with her?' Dale's brows peaked quizzically.

'No, they live on the family property with their father.'

'Opal's separated from her husband?'

'Divorced.'

Dale nodded, her hands resting motionless in the water for a minute. 'It's unusual for the father to keep the children, though, isn't it?'

'Mmm, but then I don't really think Opal wanted them with her, anyway,' Alma relayed ironically. 'Even if David hadn't refused to let her take them, I doubt if she would have applied for custody. It's very difficult to make believe you're younger than you actually are when you've two growing children around to constantly disprove it.'

'I see.' Dale began washing another mug absently. The information didn't exactly make Opal appear in a more endearing light. 'But she did originally come from the Gulf, I gather, if her parents are here too?'

'Oh, yes. The Worthingtons were among the earliest settlers in the area.'

So Opal had been one of *the* Worthingtons before her marriage, had she? Dale had heard of them, although she hadn't ever met them. 'And—er—how long do her visits usually last, then?' Suddenly it seemed very important for her to know.

'Normally it's only a couple of weeks,' Alma advised with a shrug. 'But it's been longer this time because of the races coming up next week, I expect.'

'It seems rather strange, though, that if she didn't like living up here she should have married a local grazier at all, doesn't it?' Dale mused.

Alma pursed her lips thoughtfully. 'Not really, when you remember the kind of life she'd led; being an only child, waited on hand and foot, and having doting parents willing to grant her every wish the moment she voiced it. It was a real case of too much, too soon, and sometimes I feel quite sorry for her. By the time she was eighteen, marriage was about the only thing left she hadn't tried, and although it was becoming apparent, even then, that she had a taste for the high life, it hadn't yet reached the stage of her wanting to leave the district. Besides, having come from a pastoral family I think she just naturally expected to marry into another one.' Pausing, she half laughed humorously. 'Even if it wasn't quite the family everyone else had anticipated.

'How do you mean?'

'Well, we all thought it was Corey Tavener she had her sights set on. For a while there it seemed as if you never saw one without the other, and then suddenly out of the blue, Opal's engagement to David Bryson was announced. I tell you, you could have knocked us all down with a feather!'

Another instance of Corey's liking to play, but not to pay, perhaps? speculated Dale sardonically. Not that Opal appeared to bear any grudges, however, if one judged by her greeting this morning! another thought swiftly followed the first.

'Maybe he's just not the marrying kind,' she offered in assumed indifference, curious to see the other woman's response.

'You're probably right,' conceded Alma readily—a shade too readily for her listener's liking. 'Especially since, from what I hear, no one's even yet managed to get him to the altar.'

'Not even Wanda Gilchrist!' The dry retort slipped out before Dale could stop it.

'Oh, you've heard about that, have you?' The corners of Alma's mouth curved obliquely. 'Well, I wouldn't put too much credence in that story, if I were you.'

There it was again! That tacit defence of Corey. 'You think Wanda was lying when she said Corey was the father of her child?' Dale probed cautiously.

'What I really think is that the whole matter should be allowed to rest in peace,' Alma returned with a sigh. 'Although now that Corey's returned, I guess that's just not possible, is it? You're not the only person I've heard mention the matter during this last week.'

'I'm sorry.' Dale hunched one shoulder deprecatingly, and bent to scrub more vigorously than was necessary at a milk jug. 'I suppose I really shouldn't have asked. It's none of my business.'

'As much yours as mine,' her companion allowed, chuckling. 'I've no doubt you're as intrigued by the whole affair as everyone else hereabouts. So to answer your question . . .' She sighed again.

'You don't have to if you'd rather not,' Dale cut in quickly, but secretly hoping the reverse.

'No, it's all right, love.' Alma patted her on the arm with a plump, reassuring hand. 'I was only huffing because of my own thoughts. You see, I happen to like

Wanda, I always have, *but* . . .' she heaved an even heavier breath this time, 'even though I felt there might have been a chance she was telling the truth in the beginning, I'm sorry to say that as the years have passed, I've very definitely come to believe otherwise.'

'Why?' There didn't seem to be a less blunt way of asking.

'You've seen young Reuben, haven't you?'

'Well, y-yes,' Dale stammered, not quite sure just what was being implied. 'Although only as he passes the hotel on his way to and from school, not up close.'

'But close enough to see he's an ash blond, for a start!'

Now she understood what Alma had been getting at. 'Oh, yes, but then the majority of kids at his age are fair,' she felt obliged to point out.

'Not the Taveners!' Alma shook her head decisively, meaningfully. 'Believe me, I can remember when there were a lot more of that family around Karraparinka than there are now, and not one of them—or any of the children they produced—ever had anything but jet black hair and olive skin from the day they were born.'

Dale chewed the statement over in her mind contemplatively. Wasn't that the very first thing she herself had noticed about Corey? How dark his colouring was? 'Even so, wasn't Corey's mother a redhead? I mean, they're usually always light-skinned, and perhaps that could account for Reuben's fairness.'

'Since it didn't account for anything of the kind in her own son, somehow I doubt it,' Alma disagreed. 'The more so, really, considering Wanda herself is a brunette too. Besides, quite apart from the boy's complexion, as far as I can see he doesn't have a single solitary Tavener feature either. In fact, there's been times of late when I've found myself wondering if he doesn't remind me of . . .'

'Someone else entirely?' put in Dale helpfully, guessing the reason for Alma's sudden halt had been due to a reluctance to mention any particular name.

'Mmm, that's about it,' the older woman acceded gratefully. Then she caught Dale completely unprepared by promptly qualifying, 'Of course I could be wrong. That's why I've never said anything before this. It's just a feeling I have, that's all, coupled with the knowledge that no Tavener ever had such pale blue eyes or such fair skin tones.'

'I see,' Dale acknowledged quietly, although her thoughts were nowhere near as calm. They were racing tumultuously!

Had she misjudged Corey, then, after all? If what her Uncle Irwin had said was the truth, Alma wasn't the only person to have doubts regarding Corey's part in the matter. A feeling of relief swept through her at the thought. Not that it concerned her either way, of course, but for some unknown reason she hadn't wanted him to be guilty of such heartless behaviour.

However, if Corey wasn't the responsible party, then who was? her thoughts pushed on inexorably as the washing up came to a finish—temporarily, at least— and she thanked Alma for her help. If the older woman's theory was correct, it was most likely someone with very light colouring . . . so just who would fit into that category in Karraparinka?

Not unnaturally, the first person to come to mind was Kurt, but with an inward smile, she immediately discounted him. After all, she already knew from firsthand experience that he didn't particularly care for

Wanda, and her earlier surmise that his dislike had been brought about by Wanda being responsible for Corey's having to leave town seemed even more relevant now if he'd also believed his stepbrother had been falsely accused.

So who else had fair hair and fitted in the most likely age group? Dale's forehead puckered with concentration, but before she could recall anyone definite, a stray reflection intruded. Kurt couldn't possibly have known Corey wasn't responsible, otherwise he would have spoken up, wouldn't he? Although, if it came to that, why hadn't Corey himself denied it? And that, she sighed dispiritedly, was the stumbling block to all their theories and suppositions. Surely no one silently accepted banishment from their home for something they hadn't done!

'Hey, Peg! They think they might be on to something!' Karl's excited voice riveted everyone's attention as he suddenly burst into the kitchen. 'Would you know if Mickey took anything with him yesterday? They've found a toy koala out at Horseshoe Yard.'

It was heartbreaking to watch the first flush of rising hope on Peggy's face give way to inconsolable disappointment as she shook her head dejectedly. 'He lost that about a month ago when his father took him with him to yard some heifers,' she revealed, sounding close to tears.

Karl shifted uncomfortably, his expression sympathetic. 'I'm sorry. I—I guess I'd better let them know,' he murmured awkwardly, and made good his departure almost as swiftly as he had his entrance, and leaving those remaining to try and take Peggy's mind off her sorely dashed hopes.

A short time later, when that generally regarded

panacea for just about every ill—a pot of tea—had been brewed, Dale took a mug out to Karl and each of his companions and stayed for a few minutes to listen to the various messages being relayed between the searching parties. Although interesting, it was nevertheless disheartening to hear such negative reports being made—in this situation, no news definitely wasn't good news—and with a sigh she retraced her steps to the homestead, only to find herself confronted by Opal as she mounted the front steps.

Smartly turned out in cream linen slacks and matching silk blouse, the older woman leant idly against one of the verandah roof supports, her gaze seemingly fixed to the lighted end of the cigarette held between perfectly manicured fingers.

'So what were you doing earlier? Trying to hedge your bets?' Her narrowing blue eyes abruptly locked with unexpectant violet as she sarcastically jeered the last.

'I don't know what you mean,' replied Dale with an explicit shrug that said she wasn't interested either.

'I mean your shameless play for Corey when you thought no one was looking!' Opal was only too willing to enlighten her in biting tones. 'You're certainly doing your best to ensure Tavener's Bridge doesn't slip through *your* fingers, aren't you? If one brother doesn't inherit, then the other will, and little Miss Freeman obviously means to be in there with a chance whichever way it goes!'

So much for hoping there had been no observers, thought Dale ruefully. She should have known Opal wouldn't have let Corey out of her sight that quickly. Not when she'd so obviously been anxiously waiting

for him to arrive. As for the woman's distasteful in-
sinuations . . .

'Apart from the fact that I can't see what business it
is of yours in any case, I'm sorry to have to disappoint
you, but I'm really not the least bit interested in
Tavener's Bridge,' she advised on a sardonic note.
'Anyway, I understood Corey's sole reason for returning was because his father had been ill, not because he
wanted to make a claim for his inheritance.'

'Oh, it wasn't *his* motives I was questioning . . . just
yours!' retorted Opal with pointed emphasis. 'And don't
think I'm going to fall for that transparent "I'm not
interested" routine either! That doesn't fool me at all.
If you haven't got an eye on the property, then why
were you making up to him so brazenly?'

'I wasn't,' Dale denied in mocking accents as she
took a step past the other woman. 'If you'd bothered
to spy a little more closely, you would have seen it was
Corey kissing me, not the other way around.'

'You expect me to believe that?' Opal exploded derisively, and dug her fingers into Dale's arm to stop
her when she would have resumed walking. 'Why would
he want to become involved with a nobody like you?'

Shaking free of the pinching hold, Dale only held
on to her rising temper with difficulty. 'I suggest you
ask him that if it intrigues you so much!'

Opal suddenly laughed, maliciously. 'I won't have
to, because on second thoughts, it isn't hard to guess.'
Her protruding blue eyes measured the younger girl
assessingly from head to toe. 'I suppose you could hold
a certain attraction if a man was only interested in a
physical liaison, and since Corey already knows you've
caught Kurt's interest, then I expect he could find it
tempting to cut out his stepbrother.'

'Why?' Dale struggled to keep her voice even, both as a result of Opal's denigrating remarks, and because the suspicion that Corey might be using her in some game of his own had occurred to her too—dismayingly.

'Why not, when that miserable weasel is doing his damnedest to take what's rightfully Corey's?' Opal sneered.

'Kurt is no such thing! Nor is he trying to take anything of Corey's either!' Dale found herself defending her boy-friend on the same point for the second time that day. 'It's not his fault Jack Tavener disowned his son!'

'Isn't it?'

'And just what's that supposed to imply?'

'That there's quite a number of us who believe he knew more about what was happening than he ever let on, and that he could have made some effort to prevent Black Jack carrying out his threat! But no,' she snorted contemptuously, 'there wasn't a sound out of dear old Kurt. It was in his best interests to keep quiet, wasn't it?'

'That's pure speculation!' Dale flared hotly. 'Besides, what could he have said when Corey himself was refusing to say anything? For all you know, he may have been protecting him with his silence.'

'Protecting himself, more like!'

'Why would he need to? It was Corey who was in trouble.'

'Happily for Kurt!'

'That's unfair!' Dale protested indignantly, vehemently. 'The same as every one of your other unfounded assertions has been! You can't prove any of them, and I've no intention of standing here listening to you blacken Kurt's name just because you apparently don't happen to like him.' She started walking away again.

'Then if you're so loyal to him, I suggest you just stick to him in future! But keep your hands off Corey, you mercenary, scheming trollop!' Opal hissed after her.

Dale stiffened angrily at the deliberate insult, but there was no sign of any irritation on her face when she half turned to look over one shoulder, only a taunting expression.

'Why, are you afraid a little competition might make your attempts to ensnare him yourself for the second time round even less successful than they apparently were the first?' she couldn't resist gibing, and kept walking.

'Oh, yes, you think you're pretty smart now, don't you?' Opal spat, hurrying behind her. 'I just wonder how clever you'll look, though, when it gets back to Kurt how you've been carrying on with his stepbrother in his absence. And it will get back to him, rest assured of that, because I'll make certain it does! So how cocky do you think you'll be then, eh?' She laughed spitefully. 'You could even find you've well and truly fallen between the horse and cart and missed out on Tavener's Bridge altogether, couldn't you?'

'Quite possibly,' Dale agreed with a careless shrug, glad they were nearing the kitchen which would free her from Opal's unwanted and undivided attention. 'But as it never figured in my plans in the first place, I don't expect it would worry me greatly.' Of course, a confrontation with Kurt over the matter could be something else again! she admitted with an inward grimace.

A point which didn't escape Opal either, it seemed, as she proposed smugly, 'And breaking up with Kurt wouldn't worry you either, I suppose.'

With her hand reaching for the flyscreen door, Dale aimed a disdainful look in her direction. 'Once again, I can't see that that's any of your business, Opal!' she retorted coolly, and had swept into the kitchen before the tight-faced woman could say another word.

As Don Chatfield had forecast, the temperature climbed rapidly all morning, and when the hot and dusty search parties began filtering back to the homestead at lunchtime there was an even greater sense of urgency about them as they hosed down freely sweating horses before hastily disposing of the steaks and sausages the women were cooking and downing copious quantities of tea. Although no one spoke of it, they were all well aware that if Mickey White hadn't located water himself, then his ultimate survival could depend on their finding him that afternoon.

Having covered as far as they believed a four-year-old could reasonably have travelled to the north or east during the morning, they planned a concerted effort to the south and west for immediately after they had eaten. With such a large area to search they were more likely to be successful if they weren't strung too far apart, otherwise it was possible they could miss him altogether. In the tall, dry grass, a child of that age didn't present much of an outline, and especially not if he should happen to be sitting or lying down.

During the meal, Dale and Alma were confined to the kitchen, busily ensuring there was a steady supply of clean plates and mugs. Nevertheless, Opal was conspicuous by her absence from the minute the first of the men began arriving back until they left again, and

Dale didn't need to be omniscient to know just whose company the woman would be sharing.

The two other children in the White family, who had been in the charge of an older daughter of Alma's all morning while they participated in their School of the Air lessons, also put in a brief appearance for lunch. But even they were subdued, for instead of bounding out of the schoolroom in their usual high spirits, they immediately sought their mother for news with joyless, anxious faces, as if they too were as conscious of the seriousness of the situation as were the adults.

'Well, since they didn't find him this morning, it's obvious Mickey must have gone south or west, so they're bound to find him this afternoon,' said Vida Hawke, one of Peggy's nearest neighbours, in an encouraging tone as soon as the men had departed once more.

'Of course they will!' endorsed Alma above the murmur of similar comments. 'It's only a matter of time.'

But as the long afternoon hours dragged past and there was still no heartening news, even the most optimistic of them couldn't competely hide their increasing fears. Conversation was only desultory, and by the time the vermilion ball of fire that was the sun started to slide towards the horizon, it was almost nonexistent as they all evaded each other's eyes lest they should discover in them a mirror for their own secret apprehensions.

Peggy was listlessly beginning to see about preparing some dinner for the children when the sound of booted feet racing along the verandah caught their attention, and for the second time that day Karl rushed into the room, but with a grin splitting his face from ear to ear on this occasion.

'They've found him!' he wasted no time in exclaiming exultantly.

'Oh, thank God!' gasped Peggy fervently, and sinking into a chair did what she had avoided all day—burst into tears.

'How is he? Is he okay?' asked both Alma and Vida simultaneously.

'Well, there's apparently some sunburn, dehydration, and quite a number of scratches and grazes, but thankfully none of them are too extreme,' Karl relayed happily.

'And whereabouts was he?' Peggy looked up to enquire, recovering slightly.

Karl hunched one shoulder somewhat sheepishly. 'Er—to be honest, I was in such a hurry to tell you, I forgot to ask.'

'So you don't know how long it will be before they're back?' someone else hazarded.

'Oh, yes,' he nodded quickly. 'They said most of them would take about an hour and a half, but Bill's bringing Arnold and Mickey back in the four-wheel-drive, so they should be here much sooner.'

'Right! Well, come along, ladies, there's work to be done.' Jumping to her feet, Opal summarily took charge again. 'Karl, you'd better bank up the barbecue. Everyone will need to be fed before they start for home,' she went on briskly. 'And Alma, since you and your offsider,' which Dale took to mean herself, 'have nothing to do at the moment, you can start taking the plates, utensils, etcetera, outside to the table.'

And so it continued, Dale noted wryly, until everyone had been given something to do—except Opal, of
course—and the homestead once more became a hive
of bustling activity.

CHAPTER SIX

THINKING back over the joyful reunion that had taken place between tearful mother and tired, thirsty, and hungry son only a few hours before, Dale smiled happily to herself in the darkness as the Land Rover with Corey at the wheel—he had elected to drive despite her assertions that he must have been a good deal more tired than she was—headed back towards Karraparinka.

'Well, at least all's well that ends well,' she sighed in relief. 'Although I can't really say I'd like to go through another day like today. When it started to get dark and there was still no word, the atmosphere back at the homestead was so strained you wouldn't believe it.'

'Oh, yes, I would,' Corey claimed expressively. 'None of us were exactly what you would call relaxed either, and it was really only a fluke that we heard his muffled crying when we did.'

'Mmm, fancy him crawling into a hollow log like that,' she mused with a shudder for what the consequences could have been. It seemed that some time earlier in the day Mickey had been distracted by a large lizard and when the reptile had disappeared into an old log he had squeezed in after it and become securely wedged in the process. 'I bet he never does that again. The poor little thing must have been frightened to death!'

'He was certainly glad to be rescued, I can tell you that,' Corey half laughed expressively. 'But at least it might curb his wanderlust for a while.'

'For ever, I should hope!'

'That remains to be seen, I guess.' Silent for a moment, he slanted her a brief glance. 'Apart from the tension, though, how was your day?'

Since Opal had commandeered his attention and done nothing but whisper in his ear almost from the minute he had returned to the homestead, this was more or less the only time Dale had spoken to Corey, and she wondered if there wasn't more to his remark than there appeared.

'Much as I expected,' she shrugged noncommittally. Then, with a studied nonchalance, 'Did you know that Opal's divorced now?'

He nodded his confirmation negligently. 'So I heard. I might add, I also heard you two had more words to say to one another.'

'Well, you could hardly expect us to completely ignore each other. We had to talk sometimes or it would have looked most peculiar.' She purposely misunderstood him.

'I wasn't referring to general words, I was meaning specific ones,' he elucidated drily.

'Oh, such as?' she queried, outwardly innocent, but inwardly watchful. Just what had Opal said to him during those whispering sessions? If he knew of their altercation there was only one person who could have told him.

'Your telling her to stay out of your way because, by one means or another, you didn't intend to lose out on Tavener's Bridge.'

If she hadn't been so incensed at Opal's duplicity, Dale might have laughed—it was preposterous to even think she would have said anything of the sort, and especially to her of all people—but as it was, the cooling tone she could detect in his voice had her responding with resentful facetiousness.

'Oh, is that what I said?' She fixed him with a wide-eyed and gibing look. 'You're sure it wasn't more to the effect that she should keep her hands off *you*?'

'Why? Do you recognise those particular words as being more factual?'

'Oh, without a doubt! They sound distinctly familiar,' she mocked. 'Though, as I said, I'm sure Opal's already told you that.'

'I believe she did mention something of the kind,' he averred slowly.

'Well, there you are, then!' Dale shrugged flippantly. 'All your suspicions regarding my previous inquisitiveness have been vindicated, haven't they? It was obviously nothing but a cover for my mercenary ambitions!'

'Which you just had to gloat about to Opal, of course?'

'Yes—well, I wouldn't have wanted her harbouring any false hopes where you were concerned, now would I? That could have had a disastrous effect on my plans,' she continued in the same self-deprecating fashion.

'I see,' he acknowledged expressionlessly. 'The idea being that you attach yourself to whoever gets the property, is that it?'

'Why not?' she countered pertly. That was the way Opal had apparently seen the matter. 'A girl has to think of her future, you know.'

'I suppose so,' Corey allowed with such unanticipated equanimity that Dale could only blink at him in surprise.

She had just been waiting for him to say something,

anything, derogatory or contemptuous with regard to her supposed intentions and she would have enjoyed telling him, in no uncertain terms, just what the true facts of the matter really were. However, his seeming unconcern had now taken the wind out of her sails somewhat, and perplexed furrows began to make an appearance across her forehead.

'Is—is that all you've got to say?' she enquired hesitantly, disbelievingly.

'Hmm . . . for the moment.'

Annoyed at being deprived of the opportunity to retaliate as she would have liked, Dale eyed him with a belligerent gaze. 'Meaning?' she demanded.

Corey flexed one broad shoulder impassively. 'Exactly what I said.' Topaz eyes swung to meet hers fleetingly. 'Unless, of course, there's something you wish to add on the matter.'

Dale's chin rose defiantly. 'No, nothing that I can think of,' she denied, and turning away, sought a more comfortable position as if preparing to sleep for the remainder of the trip.

If he wanted to believe Opal's venomous tale, then let him! she decided acrimoniously. Why should she care what he thought of her, anyway?

On reaching the hotel, Dale had headed straight for a shower and then bed. In the Land Rover most of her sleep had been feigned, despite the various activities and tensions of the day beginning to take their toll, but when she awoke the following morning, feeling considerably refreshed, it was with a sigh of satisfaction in knowing that the day before hadn't been total failure. At least Mickey had been found.

No sooner had she dressed and breakfasted, how-

ever, than she immediately began to wonder if she
wasn't about to have another inauspicious day, for as
soon as she reached the public lounge on her way to
the bar she found Kurt waiting for her with a thunder-
ous look on his face.

'So you weren't interested in my stepbrother, eh?'
he didn't waste any time in charging wrathfully. 'I
should have known you'd be no different from the
rest!'

Mention of Corey had Dale's facial muscles tighten-
ing in dismay. Good lord, had Opal made good her
threat already? 'Whatever are you talking about?' she
asked, trying to sound innocently amused and wanting
to hear exactly what he had to say before committing
herself.

'You know damned well what I'm talking about! It
was all over the air waves yesterday evening about
Corey's and your budding romance!' he railed.

'Our *what*?' she gasped jerkily. Somehow she suspected that wasn't quite how Opal had intended the
information to be taken. 'Oh, how r-ridiculous!'

'Is it?' he thrust his angry face forward to sneer ran-
corously.

'Well, of course it is!' she asserted in an urgent voice.
'I don't know who could have started such a
rumour,'—not much, she didn't!—'but they're wrong,
believe me! Quite wrong! There's absolutely nothing
between Corey and myself.'

'No?' he countered once more, and in just the same
scathing tone. 'Then perhaps you'd better tell him that,
because he told me something quite different!'

'Y-you've already spoken to Corey about it?' Dale's
eyes closed in despair.

'Yes, I confronted him about it!' he grated between

clenched teeth. 'And his answer makes a liar out of you, I can tell you that, you two-faced little bitch!'

'How do you mean?' she quizzed faintly, dreading to know the worst, and too perturbed to take exception to his vilification.

'Because, according to him, the pair of you are on the point of becoming engaged!'

Dale stared at him incredulously. Oh, God, was this some sort of macabre joke Corey and Opal had worked out between themselves? Or was he just using her in order to achieve his own ends, after all?

'Then he's lying!' she accused distractedly. 'Or—or you misunderstood him. Or more likely still, he was just having you on. But I can assure you, we are *not* almost engaged!'

Kurt hesitated, momentarily put out of stride by the conflicting stories. Then his lips thinned and he shook his head scornfully. 'Just friends, huh?' he jeered on a disparaging note. 'Then why the big love scene that apparently took place yesterday? Try explaining that . . . if you can!'

'Oh, there was no big love scene! The whole thing's been exaggerated out of all proportion!' she retorted exasperatedly.

'You deny kissing him?'

She made a deprecating gesture with her hands. 'Well—no, not exactly—but . . .'

'No, I didn't think so!' he broke in savagely, eyes glittering. 'Your whole protest's been nothing but a pack of lies, hasn't it? Well, I wish him joy of you, because I'm beginning to think I've had a lucky escape!' And with a last derisive curling of his upper lip, he turned on his heel and stormed from the room.

Indignation, disappointment, and anger all welled up

inside Dale as she watched him leave, and only seconds later she was pacing down the hall herself, intent on finding Corey! That Kurt should have believed she was deliberately two-timing him was bad enough, but that Corey should have gone to such lengths to further the idea was absolutely infuriating!

Unable to locate him anywhere at the front of the hotel, she headed towards the back and eventually discovered him seated on a stool in the kitchen, casually talking to Myra. And the fact that he did appear so relaxed and at ease did nothing to appease Dale's sense of outrage and, with a glare that should have felled him on the spot, she strode towards him determinedly.

'Morning, Myra,' she acknowledged with a brief, tight half smile as she crossed the room and came to a halt before the object of her attention, whereupon she heaved smoulderingly, 'I'd like a word with you in private, if you don't mind!'

Before he could answer, Myra had cut delightedly into the conversation. 'Oh, Dale! Congratulations on your impending engagement!' she exclaimed. 'I hope the two of you will be very happy.'

Not wanting to embarrass the woman by refusing to accept her good wishes, Dale stammered uncomfortably, 'Er—thank you, Myra, although I—I'm not quite sure congratulations are—er—actually in order as yet. I mean,' she paused, swallowing convulsively, on seeing the look of puzzlement creeping over the woman's face, 'it's not as if anything's really been settled.'

'But I thought . . .' Myra began, frowning.

'Dale just means it's more usual to have a ring to display before accepting congratulations,' inserted Corey easily, and cast his supposed intended a taunting smile. 'Isn't that right, angel?'

'Something like.' Her eyes clashed direfully with his.

Undeterred, he slid an arm around her slender waist, drawing her closer to his side. 'And that's what you wanted to see me about, is it?'

'Among other things!' she gritted between falsely smiling teeth.

'In that case . . .' He rose lithely to his feet, but kept her pinned against him. 'If you'll excuse me, Myra, we'll see you later.'

'Of course,' the older woman allowed readily and then chuckled. 'I expect you'd prefer to be on your own, in any case.'

And especially when murder was about to be committed! added Dale pungently, jerking free of his grasp the minute they were out of Myra's sight.

'What the hell do you think you're playing at, Corey, telling everyone we're engaged?' she demanded of him furiously. 'You know that nothing's further from the truth, and if you think it's amusing, then I can assure you, I don't! It's already broken up my relationship with Kurt!'

Turning left, Corey made for the side verandah and Dale followed him. 'Don't blame me, angel,' he drawled indolently. 'You were the one who said, whoever got Tavener's Bridge got you as well.'

Dale felt her jaw starting to drop with incredulity. 'Are you telling me that's what brought all this on? Some facetious remark I made last night?' she part gasped, part seethed.

'Was it facetious?' One dark brow crooked obliquely.

'Oh, of course it was!' she flared. And seeing the

amused flicker in his eyes, 'As you damned well know! The same as you're being now!'

He grinned quite openly at that. 'Perhaps it will teach you to be more circumspect with what you say in future.'

'In other words, it's just your way of paying me back for all those things I said, is it?'

'Not entirely.' His lips twitched wryly.

Amethyst-coloured eyes surveyed him suspiciously. 'Meaning?'

He hunched a heavily muscled shoulder impassively. 'I don't know what happened between you and Opal yesterday, but by the way she was going on the radio last night she sure didn't intend for you to have much of a reputation left when she'd finished, so . . . I figured an imminent engagement was the best way in which to put an end to all the speculation.'

'Oh!' Dale chewed discomfitedly at the inside of her lip. 'Then—then thank you,' she felt obliged to murmur, but selfconsciously. 'Does that mean you didn't believe what Opal told you about me yesterday, then, after all?'

Half sitting, half leaning against the verandah rail, Corey looked down at his long legs stretched before him. 'So it would seem.' Abruptly, his head lifted and he smiled rakishly, 'I told you I thought you had a soft heart, didn't I? Opal's claims just didn't tie in with that reckoning.'

With her breath catching in her throat as a result of that disarming smile, Dale struggled to at least appear all as unmoved by it as possible. 'Then thank you for that too,' she acknowledged, even more disconcertedly now as her cheeks warmed at the implied compliment. 'Although surely you could have explained the real circumstances to Kurt, instead of purposely making him think that my—my interest was now elsewhere, couldn't you?'

'I didn't consider it advisable,' he shrugged indifferently again.

'Why not?'

'Well, it would hardly look convincing if there was no change in his attitude towards you, now would it?' he charged wryly. 'Besides, can I help it if he has a suspicious mind? He was as free as I was to decide whether Opal was telling the truth or not.'

'Except that he had you as good as proving her correct by declaring there was an engagement in the offing!'

'So he did,' he acceded, but seeming to Dale to be more amused than concerned at the admission. 'But I shouldn't let it worry you. He was never right for you, in any case.'

'Oh, really?' Her eyes widened sarcastically. 'Well, if you don't mind, I'll be the one to decide that, not you!'

'You mean, his selfish refusal to join in the search for Mickey hadn't made you reconsider anyway?'

Dale dropped her gaze in consternation. Was he really able to read her thoughts that easily? It was true Kurt's uncaring attitude towards the child's plight had caused her to do some re-thinking, but at the same time some of her thoughts she most definitely didn't want him guessing at!

'E-even if it had, it was still *my* prerogative to tell him so,' she flouted, albeit not very forcefully.

White teeth gleamed in an entirely unrepentant grin. 'I just thought I'd save you the trouble.'

'While conveniently serving your own purposes at

the same time, no doubt!' she gibed in a stronger voice, and proceeded to cast him a highly provoking glance. 'So let's hope, for your sake, I don't choose to do the same to you in the future, hmm?'

Before she had a chance to move—or even realised there was a need to—Corey had snaked out a hand to thread his fingers within her curly hair and relentlessly drawn her closer. 'In what way?' he probed, but not altogether seriously, as the dancing lights in his tawny eyes showed.

Desperately attempting to disregard the effect his proximity was having on her nervous system, Dale forced herself to return his disturbing gaze with a taunting smile. 'Well, when you figure it's time for this so-called engagement of ours to come to an end, I just might not feel disposed to go along with its termination, mightn't I? In fact, if you insisted, and I *really* wanted to pay you back in your own coin, I could even feel inclined to charge you with breach of promise . . . and then what would you do?'

'You don't leave me much choice,' he remarked drily.

'And that is?' Her eyes continued to hold his audaciously.

Cupping her face between both hands, Corey smiled lazily. 'You'll find out . . . *if* and when it becomes necessary.'

Dale tried to snatch her head away but couldn't, and had to content herself with slanting her chin challengingly higher. 'You don't think I'd have the nerve to go through with something like that, do you?' she deduced mockingly, piqued at his humorously unworried reaction.

'It doesn't matter to me whether you have or not,

the result will still be the same,' he drawled.

His unperturbed nonchalance was becoming intolerable, and her desire to put him on the defensive for once had her quipping caustically, 'Meaning you'll just leave town and disappear, like you did before?'

For a time the only sound that could be heard was his deepened breathing, making Dale nervously aware of the strict self-restraint he was imposing on himself, and then one corner of his firmly shaped mouth sloped upward as he shook his head wryly.

'I think maybe I'd better start revising my opinion regarding the softness of that heart of yours, because where I'm concerned at least, you sure do have a tendency to hit below the belt, don't you, my sweet?' he accused, dropping his hands to rest them on his lean hips.

'I'm sorry,' she whispered disconsolately. The least she could have done was to give him the benefit of the doubt, the same as he'd given her, and especially when others—who obviously knew more about the affair than she did—weren't at all convinced of his responsibility in the matter, anyway. 'You're right, it was unfair, and I shouldn't have said it. As you've told me often enough before, your past—or present, for that matter—is none of my concern.'

'Not even as my fiancée-to-be?'

Reproachful eyes, pansy purple and framed by glossy, curling lashes, were turned briefly in his direction. 'Now you're just making fun of me,' she reproved. 'You know that it's not for real.'

'This is, though,' he proposed quietly as he agilely gained his feet, and in a continuation of the same smooth movement, spanned her jaw with a strong brown hand at the same time as he gently covered her lips with his own.

Instinctively, it seemed, a response flared within Dale, and before she could regain control of her emotions she found herself swaying towards him, involuntarily seeking a closer contact. When Corey's arms proved only too willing to oblige and secured her firmly against his muscular form, it was too late to pull away, and her supple body spontaneously moulded itself to him pliantly.

Lost in a haze of turbulent feeling, it was a while before she became aware of any extraneous thoughts again, but as a variety of sounds from the hotel began to penetrate her consciousness, she strained away from him embarrassedly.

'Someone will see us again,' she gasped on a ragged note.

Corey made no move to release her, nevertheless. 'Don't you think they'd expect a newly engaged couple to behave in such a manner?' he countered instead.

'Perhaps,' she admitted shakily. It was disturbing to discover she didn't really want to leave the circle of his arms. 'But *we* know we're not engaged, don't we?'

His sensuous mouth sought the vulnerable side of her throat. 'Mmm, but there's something to be said for keeping up appearances, don't you think?' he murmured deeply against the warm, sensitive skin.

Luckily, it was just the sort of remark needed to give Dale the impetus to struggle free and, catching him unawares, she did so. He might have been entitled to her gratitude for having suggested their mock-engagement as a barrier against Opal's malicious gossip, but she had no intention of providing him with an outlet for his amorous inclinations in repayment!

'Th-there is such a thing as overdoing it, however,' she stuttered, still recovering from the wayward shiver of receptiveness that had beset her with his last stirring touch. 'And—and if no one sees us, then it's rather a waste of time, isn't it?' Immediately on freeing herself she had checked to see if anyone had indeed witnessed their embrace.

'Well, I don't know that's exactly how I'd described it, but . . .' Corey wryly left the rest of his comment unsaid.

Dale averted her gaze selfconsciously, frantically searching for a change of subject. When his eyes looked at her like that she was all too ready to walk straight back into his arms again.

'Anyway,' she began somewhat breathlessly, 'you said before that the reason you told everyone we were getting engaged was because I'd stated that whoever got Tavener's Bridge got me as well. So does that mean you are going to inherit the property, after all, or—or were you just being sardonic?'

Resuming his seat on the verandah rail, Corey folded his arms across his chest, his head angling contemplatively to one side. 'Let's just say it was an educated guess,' he advised, but with such a knowing smile that she didn't doubt he could read the state of her present tumultuous feelings as effortlessly as he had earlier read her thoughts.

'Because Kurt isn't perhaps as competent as—as he should be?' she forced herself to continue.

His lips twitched ironically. 'Don't pussyfoot around, angel. Kurt is just plain *in*competent . . . and always has been, I'm afraid!'

'Honestly?' she quizzed in a still doubtful tone. 'You're not just saying that because—because you . . .'

'No, I'm not just saying that because I personally

haven't much time for him,' he came to her rescue with a ruefully smiled reassurance as he leant forward slightly, shaking his head. 'It happens to be nothing but the truth.'

'You don't think he could have improved since you've been away?'

'Not if what I saw on the way out there the other day was an example. He always did insist on indiscriminately running all the cattle together because he—incorrectly—reckoned it saved him work, but the old man will tear strips off him when he discovers what's been going on while he's been laid up. Kurt's little period in charge will have set his breeding programme back years.'

'But why would Kurt deliberately do that if he knows your father doesn't want them run that way?' she puzzled.

'Probably because of his mistaken belief that he knows best,' Corey laughed sardonically.

'And that's the reason you think your father won't leave him the property?'

'Considering how Black Jack feels about the place, I figure it's a fair assumption,' he shrugged.

'But Kurt said you'd been disowned!' she recollected with a worried frown.

'And it's on his behalf you're looking so anxious?'

'No! It's on yours, naturally!' she fired back indignantly. 'Even before we looked like—er—becoming engaged,' with a mocking smile, 'I always did think Tavener's Bridge rightfully belonged to you. No matter what you'd done,' she paused, flashing him a provoking glance from beneath the fringe of her long lashes, 'or hadn't done.' The expression of threatened reprisal that came over his features had her rushing on, although in a less goading fashion, for her own self-protection. 'But do you really think your father will have a change of heart, Corey? I mean, he's apparently such a hard, unforgiving man.'

'Hmm,' he pondered reflectively. 'I guess he was at times.'

'*At times*!' she couldn't help exclaiming in disbelief. 'According to everyone else, it was *all* the time!'

'Except they don't happen to know him quite as well as I do.'

'Kurt does, and he certainly doesn't agree with you!'

'But then Kurt, if you'll pardon me for saying so, wouldn't know how to handle the old man in a million years,' he relayed drily.

'Neither did you, apparently! He disowned *you*! At least Kurt hasn't managed to get that far on the wrong side of him yet!'

To Dale's surprise, that made him laugh—a low, vibrant sound that sent warm waves of feeling rolling down her spine. 'But only, I suspect, because Black Jack isn't particularly concerned about him.'

'You mean he's only especially lousy to those he likes?' she quipped acidly. 'Wow! He must really have *loved* you, to have thrown you out!'

'Uh-uh!' Corey shook his head lazily in veto. 'He didn't throw me out. I left.'

'That isn't how Kurt tells it.'

'Oh, I admit I was given an ultimatum,' he conceded with a rueful tilt to his lips. 'But the choice was still mine.'

'Some choice!' she sniped.

'But a choice, nonetheless, and probably a fair one from his point of view.'

Dale rubbed a hand across her forehead in bewilderment. 'Do you please have a cigarette? I feel I need something!' she owned plaintively. 'I don't know whether you're confusing me, or I'm confusing myself, but confused I definitely am!'

'About what?' Corey quizzed in an amused voice as he extracted two cigarettes from the packet in his shirt pocket, lit them, and handed one across to her.

'Thank you,' she acknowledged gratefully, and drawing deeply on it, expelled the smoke in a slow stream. 'Well, for a start, the impression you give of your relationship with your father is totally different from everyone else's, you know.'

'Which is only to be expected, I guess,' with a neg-ligent flexing of one shoulder.

'Yes, but even Kurt said the two of you used to argue all the time.'

'Mmm, but then I never said he was an easy man to live with either,' he half laughed wryly. 'We certainly had our disagreements. I suppose we were too similar in a number of ways not to.' The slanting curve of his mouth became more pronounced. 'We can both exhibit an excess of pride at times, and we both have an intense dislike for being stood over.'

'And is that why you left without saying anything? Because he was attempting to stand over you with his ultimatum?' she ventured curiously.

For a moment he didn't answer as his eyes took on a musing look, then he gave a rueful grin and revealed, 'Granted, I was so flamin' annoyed at the time I was capable of doing anything, but no,' both his expression and his voice hardened abruptly, 'it was mainly for other reasons that I left.'

'Such as?' she dared to probe, but in a somewhat more cautious tone than she had been using. That

sudden change in his demeanour had been very notice-
able.

The old, familiar taunting look at least returned to
his eyes. 'What makes you think I'm about to discuss
them with you?'

'Well . . . you did sort of imply that as your fiancée-
to-be I was entitled to know something of your affairs,'
she reminded him, winsomely persuasive.

'You already know more than most,' he retorted in
dry accents. 'And as for a fiancée's rights, I could point
out that there are some of a generally accepted physical
kind too, angel.'

Dale flushed hotly—not so much as a result of his
words, but of the mental pictures that involuntarily
flooded her mind. She found the thought of Corey
making love to her had an extremely tantalising attraction, but one that was perturbingly difficult to dispel.
When she did so eventually, she took a steadying draw
on her cigarette and then shrugged with as much nonchalance as she could muster.

'Fortunately, they don't apply in our case, though,
do they?' she half smiled sweetly.

'I just thought I'd mention it.'

Although his face might have been innocently
composed, his honey-brown eyes were something else
again, and the lazy devilry they contained set Dale's
heart pounding wildly, even as her lips started to curve
with grudging humour.

'Any woman who became engaged to you, Corey
Tavener, would have to be out of her mind! You are
the most tormenting male I've ever met, and I bet you
were a positive monster as a child too!' she charged
chaffingly.

'You're sounding like my mother again,' he mocked.

Mention of Yvette Tavener had Dale's smile fading and her eyes clouding sadly. 'Does—does your father really blame you for her death, Corey?' she just had to ask, no matter how reluctantly.

'Who told you that?' To her relief his tone was more curious than anything else.

'I forget,' she shrugged, mindful of her promise to her uncle not to divulge the source of her information. 'Why, isn't it true?'

With one last draw on his cigarette, Corey flicked the butt over the rail to the bare earth below and watched as the burning tip died. 'Yes, it's true,' he confirmed. 'Although probably not as much as he blames himself.'

Dale couldn't keep her astonishment from showing. That was certainly different from what her Uncle Irwin had said! 'But I was told . . .'

'Too much, by the sound of it,' he cut in ironically. 'Don't you know you shouldn't listen to hearsay?'

'Well, how else was I supposed to find out? Until this morning, every time I've asked you, you've either refused to tell me or suggested I should ask Kurt!'

'So what makes you think you're entitled to know, anyway?'

Dale stubbed out her own cigarette in an ashtray on a nearby table. 'Everyone else does,' she grimaced moodily.

'Or thinks they do, apparently,' he amended in a wry drawl.

'Well then, if they're so wrong, why did you stay away for eight years? Or is that classified information too?' she gibed.

'If you want to put it that way,' he was willing to agree, tauntingly.

'All right, I apologise for having asked!' she flared quite unapologetically. 'Keep it a big secret then, if that's what you want.'

'Thank you.' He inclined his dark head mockingly.

Dale stared at him helplessly, and feeling inexplicably close to tears as her resentment suddenly deserted her. Wasn't she ever going to learn that Corey had absolutely no intention of sharing anything but the most basic of information with her? Or perhaps more importantly, wasn't it also time she realised he had no reason to?

From inside the hotel, raised voices abruptly penetrated her dismal reverie and she recognised them as belonging to her uncles.

'As the eldest, of course it's my prerogative!' she heard Lester claim.

'Well, I can't see what age has got to do with it at all!' came Irwin's retort. 'I think we should draw for it.'

'Have a draw to see who gives the bride away? I've never heard of such a thing!' Lester expostulated.

'Maybe not, but at least that's the fairest way of deciding. She's my niece too, you know!'

'Oh, my God!' Dale turned aghast eyes skywards, her former musings temporarily forgotten. 'You know what they're discussing, don't you?' she queried of Corey almost accusingly.

'Mmm,' looking somewhat amused.

'Well, what am I going to tell them? I can't let them continue arguing over an engagement that isn't even real!'

'Oh, I don't know,' he grinned indolently. 'It probably makes a nice change for them from the colour scheme of the hotel, or how many people will be needed on the beer stall at the races this year.' The latter having been the latest bone of contention between them.

He wasn't being very helpful, and she glared at him vexedly. 'It isn't funny, Corey!' she censured. 'I don't like the idea of deceiving them, or—or everyone else, if it comes to that.'

'You'd rather have your reputation in shreds?' One well-defined brow arched eloquently.

'Compared with pretending to be engaged to you, I'm beginning to think that could have been far preferable!' she goaded dulcetly, and then fled for the doorway while she was still able. A certain glint in his eyes had advised her it was prudent.

CHAPTER SEVEN

UNTIL Kurt managed to get a lift back to Tavener's Bridge late the following afternoon, Dale felt her deception hanging over her especially heavily, for although she could have wished he had had a little more faith in her, simultaneously she couldn't help feeling extremely guilty for not revealing the truth to him.

However, once he had departed and the hotel began to fill with new arrivals as the races drew near, most times she was too occupied to allow the matter to dwell in her mind for long, and by the end of the week she found she was beginning to accept the situation, as well as the ensuing congratulatory wishes, with an equanimity that not only surprised her but disconcerted her a little too.

She didn't want to feel comfortable in the role Corey had chosen for her because she feared it could all too easily become one she wouldn't want to relinquish. She had hoped that the more she knew about him, the more able she would be to treat him with a casual impassivity, but unfortunately it seemed just the opposite was taking place. The better she came to know him, the greater was the effect he had on her emotionally, and that was something she wasn't quite sure just how to combat.

On the morning of the first day's races, Dale showered and dressed hurriedly in one of the cool cotton shifts she kept for working in, knowing that Myra and her daughter, Eileen, would be needing all

the help they could get now that every bedroom in
the large old building was filled to capacity and all the
verandahs, save the one nearest the private quarters,
had been made over into extra sleeping areas. Even
though her uncles had employed another two girls for
the occasion, there was still a tremendous amount of
work to be done before any of them could begin thinking of heading for the red dirt racecourse on the out-
skirts of town where a satellite tent city had sprung up
over the last few days as all those visitors who hadn't
accommodation in town made camp.

Eventually, though, as the hours moved on, it was at
last possible to see an end to all that required doing,
but as the hectic pace slackened, Dale found a nervous
tension overtaking her as her thoughts turned re-
peatedly to less impersonal matters. Would Jack
Tavener be coming in to the races today as Corey apparently expected, and as Kurt had as good as predicted? And just what was his reaction likely to be on
seeing his son after such an interval? Would he be
pleased or otherwise? Welcome him home, or refuse to
acknowledge him?

She was worried about their meeting, even if Corey
wasn't! In fact, when he'd left just after breakfast in
company with Don Chatfield and Ferris Broadbent in
order to lend a hand with the arrangements out at the
racecourse, she had wondered just how he could have
appeared so unconcerned at the prospect, she recalled.
There had been absolutely nothing in his demeanour
to suggest that today was likely to be any different from
all those that had preceded it since he had been in
Karraparinka.

Now, every time she heard a vehicle door slam outside
the hotel, Dale couldn't resist looking to see if it

heralded Jack Tavener's arrival. Of course, it was
always possible he would go straight to the racecourse,
she realised, but even so, whenever the sounds of a
new arrival reached her ears she continued checking to
see who it might be.

The first race was due to start just before lunch—
luckily, from the hotel staff's point of view—because
that meant none of the guests would be returning for
the midday meal but would instead be purchasing it
from one of the various barbecue stalls which had been
erected at the track, and thereby leaving them free to
join the gathering.

Since her uncle Lester was remaining behind at the
hotel, just in case anyone should wish to avail themselves of its hospitality, and her uncle Irwin was
already manning the beer stall at the track, after
changing into a more suitable dress but leaving her
shapely tanned legs bare as she donned a pair of
strappy, high-heeled sandals, Dale accompanied Myra
and Eileen and the other two girls as they walked down
the street and across to the racecourse.

A race was due to start almost as soon as they arrived
and Myra, apparently being something of a frustrated
punter, immediately disappeared among the swarm-
ing crowd, heading for the nearest bookmaker's stand
with her daughter following not far behind. For a
moment Dale stood staring at the gaily dressed throngs
of people milling about her. The size of the crowd had
taken her aback a little—she really hadn't envisaged
there being quite so many present—and as she and the
two younger girls began making their way towards the
rather time-worn rails that surrounded the track, she
wasn't altogether surprised when thy became separated
somewhere along the way. Trying to re-locate them

proved futile, though, as everyone else began heading in the same direction a few seconds later—as was attempting to see anything over the heads of those already lining the rails, she soon discovered—and with a wry smile she turned on her heel and decided to make for her uncle Irwin's stand instead.

This, at least, was easier to reach, although by no means deserted, and her relative was busily engaged in serving when she got there.

'How's it going?' she smiled at him fondly when he had a moment's respite. 'Do you need any help?'

'No, thanks, love. You have a good time and enjoy yourself,' he declined her offer with a quick shake of his head. Looking down below the counter and slightly to his left, he went on with a grin, 'Although you might not believe it, I do have a couple of helpers here, even though they seem to be making heavy weather of it at the moment.'

'Oh?' Her winged brows peaked curiously as she peered across the counter. She hadn't realised there were others with him.

'Well, I must say some people's gratitude is nigh to overwhelming, isn't it, mate?' drawled Don chaffingly to his companion as they dragged cartons of cans out from beneath the bench and proceeded to empty them into a couple of bathtubs filled with ice, this having been collected during the morning from the prawn trawler base on the coast of the Gulf some forty kilometres distant.

'Positively extravagant!' agreed Corey in the same bantering tone, and with a slow, lazy smile that had Dale's throat constricting.

'And when you consider the wage he's not paying us,' Don continued.

'Huh! I was under the impression I was doing *you* the honour by letting you help,' laughed Irwin, not to be outdone. 'It's not everyone I'd trust not to drink my profits on me, you know.' He fixed Corey with a meaningful glance. 'But now I suppose you're planning to run out on me, anyway, in order to escort my niece around.'

'Oh, no, I wouldn't dream of taking him away from you,' broke in Dale swiftly. Notwithstanding the fact that they were supposedly about to become engaged, she still felt extremely embarrassed when it was automatically assumed Corey enjoyed, or would want, her company. 'I can find my own way around, and—and I can see how busy you are.'

'Not right at the moment we're not,' Corey contradicted wryly, and making her wonder if he wasn't aware of just how unsure of herself he made her feel—

The sound of the caller's voice coming through the small public address system was suddenly drowned beneath a roar of cheering, indicating the end of that particular contest.

'No, but you very soon will be,' she returned excusingly, taking a few steps away, and nodding towards those groups who had already left the rails.

Corey held up a hand towards Irwin, his fingers spread wide. 'Five minutes,' he promised, smiling, and ducked under the side bench of the stall.

On reaching Dale he looped an arm across her shoulders and bent his head close to her ear. 'You'll give the game away if you're not careful, angel,' he reproved indolently. 'You're at least supposed to *act* as if you're not averse to my company, you know.'

For her own protection Dale kept her eyes to the front. It was difficult enough pretending to be unmoved by his nearness, without needlessly making it even harder for herself. 'Well, maybe I'm one of those fiancées who prefer not to show their feelings in public,' she shrugged.

'And in private?' he taunted softly.

She looked at him then, involuntarily, but promptly averted her gaze again after only a brief moment's contact with his challenging topaz-coloured gaze. 'As to that . . . when I do actually become engaged, I'll let you know,' she advised mockingly. As on previous occasions, she found sarcasm was the best—if not the only—means of defending her unruly senses. Then seeking to divert his attention, she went on hurriedly, 'I—I've been watching for your father all morning, but I haven't seen him yet. Have you?'

'Uh-uh!' His lips curved sardonically. 'But then it wouldn't surprise me if he didn't put in an appearance today at all.'

'But you expected him to, didn't you?' she frowned.

The tilt of his mouth became decidedly more pronounced. 'I expect him to arrive *some* time either today or tomorrow, but I guess you have to allow Louise at least one victory.'

'I don't follow you.' Dale shook her head perplexedly.

Guiding her around a bookmaker's stand and heading in the direction of the camping area, Corey gave a crooked grin. 'Then forget it. It's my problem, not yours.'

Dale sighed helplessly. He was back to keeping his own counsel again. 'You're a real loner, aren't you, Corey?' she mused dispiritedly. For some unknown reason the thought was depressing.

The arm about her shoulders moved slightly and his fingers began to play disconcertingly up and down the side of her neck. 'You don't think I should be where you're concerned?' he countered in a whimsical tone.

'I—I . . .' It was almost impossible to think while even that light touch could create so much havoc within her. With a deeply indrawn breath she at last managed to regain some control. 'Well, it wouldn't really hurt that much to be a trifle more explicit, would it? I mean, you were the one who mentioned your stepmother, and—and it is terribly frustrating, not to say confusing, when you only know half the story.'

To her relief his hand slid back to her shoulder. 'The whole story, I can't guarantee, even for you, angel,' he advised ruefully.

'I see.' Her head drooped defeatedly, despondently.

'I doubt it.' A forceful hand immediately tipped her face up to his again. 'I said I couldn't guarantee the *whole* story.'

'Then you'll tell me what you meant with regard to your stepmother?' she queried warily.

He flexed one muscular shoulder in a noncommittal gesture. 'I'm surprised you haven't worked that out for yourself.'

Dale paused, thoughts flitting through her mind at a furious pace. 'You think she's the reason your father might not turn up today?' she finally put forward in a tentative voice.

'It's a distinct possibility, knowing Louise.'

'But Kurt said . . .' she burst out impetuously, and then stopped, uncertain whether she would be making matters better or worse by continuing.

'Mmm?' he said watchfully. Corey obviously had no such worries.

'He—er—said it wouldn't matter whether his mother wanted you to see your father or not, because you were well aware you only had to—er—wait her out, and you'd be able to see him when he came in to the races,' she disclosed, albeit somewhat awkwardly.

Corey's jaw tightened noticeably, then relaxed into the beginnings of an unexpected smile. 'And just how did he come to volunteer all that information, might I ask?' he quizzed drily.

'I asked him, of course,' she owned, her chin lifting defiantly. 'You told me to, if you remember, after you'd refused to say why you hadn't seen your father at Tavener's Bridge that day.'

'And Kurt's reason for that was . . .?'

'That his mother knew what was best for her husband, and that she didn't know what kind of effect your sudden appearance might have on him.'

'Amongst other considerations,' came the cynical addition.

Dale nodded thoughtfully. 'Yes—well, I must admit I thought it was rather a flimsy excuse myself.'

'Did you say as much to Kurt?' His lips curved with amusement at the thought.

'Sort of,' she allowed, her own lips quirking now too.

'I bet he didn't take too kindly to that,' Corey grinned, wryly astute.

'No, not really. He snapped my head off!'

'Poor Dale,' he half laughed. 'You've been catching the flak from both directions, haven't you?'

She hunched a slender shoulder dismissively. 'At least you don't usually snap, you just close up like a clam.' And casting him an expressive glance, 'Although sometimes I think that's even harder to accept.'

'You prefer rancour?' Both his dark brows arched teasingly.

She didn't answer, just sent him another glance that

spoke even greater volumes than her previous one had done, and returned to the subject which seemed to have been preying on her mind all morning.

'But if Louise has succeeded in keeping your father away today, what's to prevent her from doing the same tomorrow too?' she asked anxiously.

'Black Jack himself! No matter what strategy she tries, he won't miss both days.'

'You sound very confident.' She only wished she could feel the same way.

'With you on my side, how can I lose?'

Uncertain whether he was making fun of her or not, Dale let it pass, choosing to ask instead a few minutes later, 'Where are we going?' They were among the campers setting up their picnic lunch tables now.

'You'll see shortly.'

With which uninformative reply she had to be content until they presently came across a family group, the children playing with friends beneath a nearby tree while their parents prepared lunch, and she recognised them instantly.

'Why, it's Peggy and Arnold!' she exclaimed pleasurably. 'And Mickey too!' as the tow-headed youngster sped past. 'I'm glad to see he appears completely recovered from his ordeal.' She flashed a wide, entrancing smile upwards.

For a time amethyst eyes became inescapably locked with tawny gold, scattering Dale's senses and making her struggle for breath as her heart began drumming a ragged beat against her ribs. Then, with an imperceptible tensing in the arm about her shoulder, Corey broke the spell.

'After all your worrying last Sunday, I thought you'd be pleased,' he said in much deeper accents than usual.

'Yes, he looked very woebegone the last time I saw him,' she acceded thickly, and stepping quickly ahead, moved out from beneath his arms as she went forward to speak to Mickey's parents.

'Here, have a seat, and I'll get you both a cup of tea,' offered Peggy as soon as she had finished greeting them.

Arnold immediately looked across at Corey with enquiringly raised brows. 'Or would you prefer something cold?' he grinned.

'No, neither for me, thanks all the same,' Corey smilingly included them both in his refusal. 'I promised Irwin I wouldn't be away long. I just brought Dale down to see you, and to show her that Mickey's apparently back to his effervescent self again.'

'Oh, yes,' Peggy confirmed happily as she poured a fresh mug of tea from the billy hanging over the campfire. 'Two days and you'd never know it happened.' Smiling her acceptance of the mug the older woman passed to her, Dale asked interestedly, 'He's suffered no ill effects from the experience, then?'

'None whatsoever, thank heavens, apart from a reluctance at present to go beyond the house paddock, but I don't think that's such a bad thing,' laughed Peggy in response. 'If he's learnt that lesson, it's done some good at least.'

Dale nodded understandingly, her eyes involuntarily seeking the little boy under discussion, and then glancing absently over the other children he was playing with. Two of them were his brother and sister; the remainder she couldn't place except for a couple she knew lived in town, and it was on one of the latter that she found her gaze concentrating the most. Reuben Gilchrist's extremely blond hair made him very conspicuous, even among his mostly fair-haired contemporaries, and she couldn't help looking up at Corey as he stood behind her chair in order to gauge whether he had noticed the child too—only to discover, however, that his gaze was fixed in another direction entirely. It was focussed squarely on herself.

'I'm sorry, but I guess I'd better get back to the stall. It's Irwin's busiest time during the lunch break. So will you be all right?' Warm honey-brown eyes surveyed her thoughtfully.

'Don't worry about Dale. We'll look after her for you,' chuckled Arnold before she could reply, and thereby negating the need for her to do so, even if she hadn't felt capable of taking care of herself.

'Thanks,' Corey smiled back. And with an encompassing, 'I'll see you all later, then,' he gave a gentle, parting tug to one of Dale's dark curls and began heading back the way they had come.

The conversation turned to more general topics after he had left, but whenever there was a pause Dale couldn't prevent her eyes from straying back to young Reuben again. Seeing him had brought Alma Fletcher's comments flooding into her mind once more, and she surreptitiously studied the child at every opportunity.

Abruptly, on one such occasion, one of the other children apparently did something to annoy him, and the infuriated look that came over his face arrested Dale's attention in shocked incredulity. Oh God, *Kurt* was Reuben's father! she suddenly realised to her horror. The evidence was too damning to ignore. In a temper, their expressions were so alike as to be indistinguishable!

A feeling of revulsion began to engulf her. No

wonder he appeared discomfited in Wanda's presence, but it wasn't on Corey's behalf, as she'd mistakenly believed, it was on his own! Just what sort of a man was he? It was bad enough that he refused to acknowledge his own child when he obviously knew the child was his, but that he should have allowed Corey to take the blame, and then stood silently by and seen him disowned for it as well, was sickening! She could also guess now why he hadn't wanted to meet his stepbrother when he first heard Corey had returned. He had probably been too embarrassed to face him!

Not that her behaviour had been exactly creditable either, she went on to muse painfully. Her taunts regarding his reputation must have rankled unbearably for Corey, and the temptation to put her in her place by disclosing all he knew about Kurt must have been very great. So great, in fact, that she doubted whether she would have been as forbearing in not divulging everything had their positions been reversed!

But now, knowing that she at least owed him an apology, it suddenly seemed imperative that she give it immediately, and replacing her mug on the table she rose swiftly to her feet, much to her companion's obvious surprise.

'I'm sorry, but I just remembered something,' she half laughed excusingly. 'I—I had a message for Uncle Irwin, but I forgot all about it when I was talking to him. I'll just go back and tell him, if you don't mind. I won't be long.'

'No, you go ahead.' Peggy waved her on her way goodnaturedly, then gave a teasing grin. 'I expect the sight of Corey put it right out of your mind. It's amazing what love can do to the memory at times!'

'I g-guess so,' Dale stammered selfconsciously, and

made good her departure before any further such comments could be made.

One particular word that Peggy's remark had instilled in her mind wasn't quite so easily left behind, though, and before she had left the camping area even, she was being swamped by her second totally unexpected revelation of the day. And this one was perhaps even more devastating than the first.

She was in love with Corey! Hopelessly, fervently, everlastingly in love with the man she was supposedly about to become engaged to for all the wrong reasons. Now she knew why she found it so difficult to play the part when he was around. She wanted the role on a permanent basis, not a temporary one!

As she neared the refreshment stands, her steps slowed and her eyes promptly sought the second one along. On finding the figure they were searching for, Dale sighed disconsolately. Not only were her feelings too shaken at the moment for her to attempt to speak to him with anything approaching composure, but there were far too many people clustered around the stall for her to do so anyway.

'Well, don't we look dejected!' A simpering voice suddenly sounded close beside her, 'What's up, Dale? Are you disappointed because Corey obviously prefers serving on the stall instead of squiring you around? Or is it just because you're not the centre of attention today?'

Giving herself time to recover some poise, Dale turned slowly to eye her elaborately dressed antagonist with as much coolness as possible. In her chiffon and pearls, Opal looked more suitably attired for Royal Randwick than an outback race meeting. 'It's neither, actually,' she denied in her most ironic tone. 'Although the only time I may have been the centre of attention since coming to Karra, I understand I have you to thank for it.'

'Oh, yes, and now you feel damned pleased with yourself, don't you?' Opal spat.

'Not particularly,' Dale shrugged. 'Should I?'

'I wouldn't, if I were you,' Opal half laughed, half sneered. 'Because I know exactly why Corey stepped in like he did, even if you don't. He always did have a stupidly quixotic streak, but you can take my word for it, he'll never marry you. Disowned or not, graziers' sons don't marry cheap little barmaids from shabby local pubs, Miss Freeman. They marry other *graziers'* daughters!' she clearly took delight in stressing. 'So perhaps you should have been content with just Kurt, after all. Since he isn't a grazier's bootlace to start with, your plans may have been more successful where he's concerned.'

'Oh, I don't know. Nothing ventured, nothing gained, as they say,' Dale returned with assumed nonchalance. Not for anything would she give Opal the satisfaction of knowing she was also well aware there would be no marriage. Quite apart from his occupation, it was all too plain Corey just wasn't the marrying kind. She forced a taunting smile on to her lips. 'And you have to admit, so far I've certainly been more successful than you ever were.'

'Bitch!' hissed Opal succinctly, venomously, her eyes glittering like splintered glass. 'You might think you're in an unassailable position now, but it won't be for long, I can assure you! My family holds a considerable sway in this district, and by the time I'm through with you, you'll wish you'd never heard of Karraparinka. Last Sunday was only a beginning, but there's more than one way to dispose of the likes of you!'

'And if those methods involve malice, deceit, and unscrupulousness, I've no doubt you know them all,' Dale retorted in a scornfully mocking voice. 'But in the meantime, if you'll excuse me, I know of far more pleasant ways to spend the afternoon than listening to you rant and rave.' And she began walking away.

'Is that so?' Opal's tone became more shrill as she grasped at Dale's arm and pulled her to a halt. 'Well, I haven't finished what I want to say yet!'

'Oh, I think you have,' Dale disputed sardonically after a hasty survey had shown they were attracting some rather curious glances from those people nearest them. 'We seem to have something of an audience already, and if you don't let go of my arm, just imagine how embarrassed you'll feel if I decide to give a de-monstration of the judo I've learnt during eight years' training and you end up lying in the dirt in all your expensive finery.'

Although Opal's grip loosened somewhat, it wasn't removed altogether as her pale blue eyes scanned the shapely figure in front of her measuringly. 'You're lying!' she finally jeered. 'What would you know about judo?'

Dale glanced pointedly at the scarlet-tipped fingers still clutching her forearm. 'It will be my pleasure to show you if you don't immediately take your hand away,' she warned.

Whether it was due to Dale's calm, self-assured gaze, or because she just wasn't quite game to put it to the test, but whatever the reason, Opal suddenly gave a partly nervous, partly pseudo-disdainful laugh and reluctantly did as she had been advised.

'I didn't let go because I thought you could do it,'

she promptly blustered. 'But because I didn't wish to be part of the spectacle you would have created by trying. I mean, that sort of public display may be acceptable for people like you, but for someone of my position it's totally abhorrent.'

'Well, don't let it worry you,' quipped Dale drily over her shoulder as she turned away. 'Believe me, your behaviour's already obnoxious enough as it is.'

Behind her, she heard Opal snarl something beneath her breath and guessed it was nothing complimentary. But then it appeared none of Opal's remarks ever were, she recalled with a rueful shaping of her mouth as she continued on her way back to the camping area. The woman seemed to think her wishes should be law—and especially where Corey was concerned!

It was almost as if she considered she had a long-standing claim on him, and although Dale had somehow managed to show a confident exterior when alleging she was his fiancée, now there was no Opal to convince it was a different matter entirely. She *wasn't* about to become engaged to Corey, was never likely to be, and as Opal had so correctly surmised, his reasons for pretending they were had been purely quixotic ones.

The thought had an aching lump settling in Dale's chest where her heart should have been, and as she made her way back to the Whites' camp it was only through sheer willpower that she was able to acknowledge greetings from those people she knew with anything like her normal spontaneity.

'Oh, there you are! I was beginning to think you might have got lost,' smiled Peggy humorously on her return. 'Is everything okay now?'

'I'm sorry?' Dale's brows drew together in a

confused expression.

'Lester's message,' Peggy elucidated with a surprised look. 'You did manage to give it to Irwin, didn't you?'

'Oh! Oh, yes,' Dale lied embarrassedly as she remembered the excuse she had given for leaving. And in order to explain her apparent forgetfulness, 'I—er—stopped to speak to a few people on the way back and I guess that must have put it out of my mind.'

What hadn't been dismissed from her thoughts, however, was the knowledge that there was no way she could continue acting the part of Corey's fiancée now that she had realised she was in love with him. She doubted she could conceal the true state of her emotions sufficiently for that, and it would be all too humiliating if he should discover just how she really felt about him when it was patently obvious that acquiring a wife—even with more impressive social connections than hers—had never been high on his list of importance.

CHAPTER EIGHT

IF possible, it was even more hectic at the hotel the following morning than it had been the day before, because there had been a dance at the local Shire Hall the previous evening which had lasted until the small hours of the morning, with the result that a considerable number of guests were in no hurry to leave their beds and so made the serving of breakfast take far longer than usual.

Although both Dale's uncles had urged her to go to the dance, she had adamantly refused, using as an excuse the fact that the hall would be unbearably hot and crowded, and that as it was no doubt their busiest night of the year they needed all the assistance they could get in the bar.

Corey, she had noted, had expressed very little concern at her decision, merely accepting it with an impassive shrug and disappearing for the rest of the evening shortly afterwards in the company of Don Chatfield and Ferris Broadbent again. Dale had reviewed his absence with conflicting emotions—relief, on the one hand, and disappointment tinged with self-annoyance, on the other. For though she was aware that the less she saw of him the easier it would be on herself, her innermost feelings unfortunately wouldn't react quite so logically, and to her despair had remained waywardly unconsoled by the lack of his presence all evening.

Immediately the last of the guests had eventually left

the dining room, Dale and Eileen swiftly began clearing the tables. Because the hotel didn't possess a dishwasher—her uncles hadn't yet managed to resolve their differences as to which particular model they would purchase—it would take them some time to complete the washing up. So although Dale wasn't planning on going to the races again herself, having offered to man the hotel for her uncles instead, she still hurried through the work as quickly as she could for the sake of Myra and Eileen, who were definitely planning another visit to the racetrack.

Finally, however, the kitchen was returned to its normal spick and span condition, and while Eileen set off to give a hand to the two other girls attending to the bedrooms upstairs, Dale headed for the public rooms on the ground floor. But as she passed the guests' lounge on the opposite side of the hall to the bar, she came to a sudden halt on seeing Corey seated on one of the sofas, talking in a low, confidential voice and holding the hand of a rather misty-eyed Wanda Gilchrist.

With her own eyes widening in shock, Dale could only stand and stare helplessly as her nails dug painfully into her involuntarily clenching hands. Then, accidentally meeting the other girl's brown-eyed gaze—Corey fortunately had his back to her—she turned away selfconsciously and hurried on to the bar, where she started rearranging tables and chairs at the same furious speed as questions kept leaping into her mind.

Could there possibly have been something between Corey and Wanda, after all? Surely there must have been, otherwise why would he now be holding her hand and talking to her in such an intimate manner?

Just because Reuben wasn't his child, it didn't mean he hadn't been interested in Wanda too, did it? In fact, perhaps that was why he had left town as he did, and even why he had never married. After discovering Wanda had been two-timing him, maybe he had been disillusioned to such an extent that he had willingly left Karraparinka and had preferred to stay well clear of the institution of marriage ever since.

And now? Dale's active brain went on inexorably. What was happening now? Were they re-living the good times of the past as they discovered their feelings for each other hadn't changed, or were they planning even better times for the future? Either way it brought no assuagement for Dale's tortured emotions and she had to catch her bottom lip between her teeth to stop its anguished trembling.

'Dale? I'd like to speak to you, if I may.'

The softly spoken words had Dale swinging to face the doorway and drawing a deep, calming breath as Wanda came into the room. 'Yes, of course,' she agreed, hunching one slender shoulder in a hopefully unconcerned fashion. Of its own volition her glance immediately travelled past the other girl. 'Is Corey with you?'

Wanda half smiled ruefully. 'No, he doesn't even know you saw us together, actually. I just thought it would be easier for us to talk without him being present, that's all.'

'Oh? What about?' tautly. Was she about to have her previous deductions confirmed?

'Well, for a start, I'd like to thank you for being so understanding when you saw us. I could see how surprised you were, and it must have taken a great deal of restraint not to have rushed in resentfully as I'm sure most fiancées would have done.'

Still wary of the turn the conversation would take, Dale made a dismissing gesture with one hand. 'Corey's still a free agent. We're not engaged yet,' she said in the same stiff tone.

'But you very soon will be, if all I hear is true,' corrected Wanda gently. 'And that's really why I wanted to talk to you. With all the resurrected gossip that's been flying around since Corey returned it must have made things very difficult for you, and I think you're entitled to know the truth about us. So, since I figured it was unlikely Corey would be revealing many details, I've taken it upon myself to . . .'

'Do you love him?' Dale cut in baldly, unable to bear the waiting any longer.

'Corey?' Much to the younger girl's surprise, Wanda appeared to spend some time considering the question. 'Mmm, I suppose I probably do,' she divulged pensively. 'Although I'm not *in* love with him, if that's what you're thinking.'

'You're not?' Dale gazed at her in bewilderment. That denial had been totally unexpected.

Wanda shook her head slowly, her expression regretful. 'No, I'm afraid I didn't use such good judgment when I fell in love. I naïvely allowed myself to be swept off my feet by someone who was willing to promise anything until he got what he wanted, and then didn't want to know me once I became pregnant.'

'Kurt?' Dale put forward tentatively.

Not bothering to deny it, Wanda asked wryly instead, 'So you've noticed Reuben's growing likeness to him, have you?'

'I did for a moment yesterday,' Dale nodded.

'Yes—well, these days the similarities are becoming

very obvious, and if you've already noticed them then I suppose before very long it's going to be extremely difficult for Kurt to continue ignoring the fact that he has a son,' Wanda sighed. She partly turned her head towards the doorway. 'It was because of Reuben that I was talking to Corey just now. I wanted to apologise for the trouble my lies caused him all those years ago. I've never had an opportunity to before.'

Relaxing a little now, Dale pulled out a chair for the older girl at one of the small tables and then took a seat herself. 'But why did you lie, Wanda?' she probed softly.

Wanda's attractive features clouded in reflection. 'Mostly out of panic, I guess. Besides . . .' her lips twisted drily, 'if you could choose between Kurt and Corey, which one would you pick? Which one *did* you pick?' She stressed the word explicitly.

Even though the circumstances in her case weren't quite as they appeared, Dale accepted the assumption silently. She had made the same choice, anyway, hadn't she?

'But I thought you said you'd fallen in love with Kurt,' she reminded Wanda doubtfully. 'Were you seeing Corey at the same time, then, too?'

'Oh, I loved Kurt all right, but I was also well aware that I didn't particularly *like* him . . . and especially when he greeted the news of my pregnancy with the information that I wasn't good enough for him to marry,' Wanda revealed with an ironic catch in her voice. 'As for Corey—well,' she shrugged fatalistically, 'I liked him, and I already knew him well because he was a mate of one of my brothers, so when he stayed at our place one night after they and some others had had a particularly heavy drinking session, I—er—made certain I was found sharing his bed the following morning.' She gave a mirthless, self-mocking laugh. 'I was very young at the time. I must have been to think Corey would fall for such a ruse, but as I said, I was in something of a panic after Kurt's hasty desertion.' Halting briefly, she worried at her lower lip with even white teeth. 'After that, of course, there was the money to be considered.'

Dale's ears pricked immediately. 'Money? What money?' she repeated, frowning watchfully.

'Pay-off money, I suppose you'd call it. To ensure I didn't change my story.'

'From Kurt?' Dale gasped.

'He may have been the one who offered it, but I never doubted there was a far sharper brain than his behind the idea,' Wanda enlightened her in a somewhat sardonic manner. 'In any case, Kurt's never had access to that kind of money.'

'Then who?' Her mind moved on logically. 'His mother?'

'Most probably,' came the nodded affirmation. 'Louise Tavener is very family—*her* family—minded, and it was certainly her sons who stood to benefit if Corey could be edged out of the picture.'

'Yet knowing that, you still didn't tell the truth?' Dale shook her head incredulously.

'By then, how could I?' Wanda lifted her shoulders in a helpless movement. 'Having originally said Corey was responsible, I could hardly turn around—no matter how much I might have wanted to—and say I'd made a mistake and that actually it was Kurt who was to blame.' She exhaled heavily. 'Anyway, to be quite honest, we needed the money. Since Corey was refus-ing to come to the aid of the party, as it were—not that I blame him, mind you—and Kurt had already made it abundantly clear he wasn't about to make any acknowledgment, then it was obvious I was going to be left, literally, holding the baby, and with six kids of his own to support on a ringer's pay my father wasn't exactly enamoured of the prospect, I can tell you! So, as it was too late by that stage to alter anything, I decided to swallow what little pride I had left and at least relieve my parents of some of their burden.'

Dale could only feel pity for the girl opposite her. In desperation, and all brought about by Kurt's worthless promises, she had misguidedly set in motion a chain of events over which she then had no control, but the guilt for which had obviously lain heavily on her during the ensuing years. And all while Kurt coolly went about his business as if he'd had nothing to do with the matter whatsoever! Nonetheless, not everything had been explained as yet.

'But why didn't Corey make any denial?' she questioned curiously. 'Surely he must have realised what his stepmother was trying to do.'

Wanda's forehead puckered in thoughtful contemplation. 'With regard to his denying it, I must say I've often wondered myself why he didn't, and the more so when his father threatened to disown him if he didn't marry me. Although, of course, no one quite knows for certain just what *was* said out at Tavener's Bridge at the time. Or at least, those who do know have made sure they kept it well and truly to themselves,' she half laughed eloquently.

'No matter what was said, I'd have thought the knowledge that his stepmother was paying you to continue blaming him would have been sufficient to make him say *something*, all the same!'

'Except that, until a few days ago, he apparently wasn't aware she had.'

Her words burst over Dale like an exploding star-shell—starkly illuminating. 'That must have been what he was referring to when he returned from trying to see his father and asked me if I'd ever experienced the feeling of being had!' she exclaimed. 'I thought he looked mad enough to cut someone's throat, and now I know why.' Her expression changed to one of acid dryness. 'Well, well, one way and another, he really was set up to take the blame for Kurt, wasn't he?'

'Mmm,' nodded Wanda miserably. 'And I feel dreadful knowing it was my fault it all happened. Especially to Corey, of all people. I must have been out of my mind!'

'With worry, by the sound of it!'

'Even so, it doesn't provide much comfort, I'm sorry to say.' Wanda's smile was filled with remorse. 'Although I am relieved I've been able to explain things to you. Since you're planning to marry Corey I thought it only fair you should know the truth.'

Dale returned her smile selfconsciously as Wanda's remark about marriage abruptly had her feeling as if she had accepted the other girl's confidences under false pretences. 'Thank you. I—I can imagine what a hard decision it was for you to make.'

Rising to her feet, Wanda made a wry face. 'Not as hard as it would have been a couple of years ago, though. Just knowing that it won't be long before everyone will be able to tell for themselves who Reuben's father is certainly seemed to make it a lot easier.'

'I suppose it would,' averred Dale meditatively as she accompanied the older girl towards the hall. 'But how do you think Kurt will react when—when it does become common knowledge?'

'Initially, with his usual bluster, I expect,' Wanda laughed drily. 'That appears to be the norm for Kurt when he finds himself in a situation he can't control. Then, after his mother has whispered a few autocratic words in his ear, he'll brazen it out by behaving as if it's beneath his dignity to have ever had anything to do with us.' She laughed again, cynically. 'As you can tell, I've been through it all before.'

'I'm sorry.' It seemed inadequate, but what else could Dale say?

'Oh, it doesn't bother me much any more. I guess I must have become used to it,' Wanda shrugged. 'Besides, nowadays I'm inclined to think he could have unwittingly done me a favour. Somehow, I think I'm better off as I am, rather than being married to Kurt.'

'You could have a point there,' Dale concurred in expressive understanding. The more she learnt about Kurt the more she was beginning to realise that to have said there were a few flaws in his character would have been an understatement!

Having said goodbye to Wanda from the verandah, Dale returned to the bar in order to finish tidying the room, and then moved on to the lounge and absently started restoring that room to order as well. Her thoughts, meanwhile, were steadfastly concentrated on Wanda's recent disclosures, together with an even more urgent awareness that an opportunity still hadn't yet presented itself whereby she could convey to Corey the apology she had intended offering him the previous afternoon.

Presently, Lester and Irwin put in a brief appearance to advise that they were on their way to the racetrack, and wishing them an enjoyable time, Dale hastily completed her work in the lounge so that she might return to the bar in order to open up for the day's trading. Not that she envisaged there being much until that evening—as had been the case yesterday—but at least with all three sets of doors open they allowed whatever cooling draughts of air that might be around to enter the already warm room and be circulated by the steadily rotating ceiling fans.

'I understand you're not going to watch the races today.' Corey's voice had her suddenly looking up in surprise to see him lean negligently against the end of the bar counter.

Recovering quickly, she shook her head. 'No, I offered to take over for Uncle Lester so he could go instead.' Then, casting him a dubious glance from beneath the curve of luxuriant lashes, 'Aren't you going either?' In actual fact, she had thought he'd left some time before.

He flexed his shoulders in a noncommittal movement that told her nothing. 'Maybe I should stay and keep you company.'

'There's no need,' she promptly denied. Feeling as she did about him, she doubted she could feign indifference to his disquieting presence for any length of time. 'A—a new batch of magazines arrived the other day, and I was planning on having a good read while the place is so quiet.'

'Okay,' he acquiesced with the same dispassion as he had the evening before when hearing of her decision not to go to the dance, and which she now found equally unsettling. 'I think I'll have a beer before I leave, though. As long as that won't prove too distracting for you,' he added, his brows lifting in lazy mockery as he retrieved a two-dollar note from the back pocket of his fawn-coloured, hip-hugging pants and laid it on the counter.

'I daresay I'll survive,' Dale retaliated in bittersweet tones, and exchanged the note for an ice-cold can in a customary holder, together with his change.

However, halfway back to where she had been standing, she stopped, ostensibly to rearrange some coolpacks beneath the counter, but actually in order to send a covert, sideways look towards the end of the bar. Of course, now was the perfect chance to make her apology, she conceded, even while biting at her lip indecisively. The only trouble was, some of the courage with which she had set out to do it yesterday afternoon seemed to have deserted her, so that now she had to compel herself to attract his attention.

'Corey?' she called in a diffident, almost inaudible voice.

'Mmm?' At first he didn't immediately look her way, but when he did it was with an unusually inflexible gaze that took her aback a little.

'I—I . . .' The sound of a vehicle door being slammed diverted her for a moment, and her eyes swung in the direction of the street. A short second later, dark and apprehensive, they flashed back again. 'Your father's here!' she advised on a somewhat shaky note.

Whatever reaction Dale had expected her announcement to produce, it wasn't the calm, almost leisurely acceptance she received as Corey merely straightened a little and queried obliquely, 'Together with Louise and Kurt?'

'I don't think so.' She shook her head swiftly, but glanced outside again just to be sure. 'At least, I can't see them.' Neither was Jack Tavener in sight any more either, she suddenly realised, and she waited expectantly, nervously, for him to appear in the bar doorway.

When he did so, she immediately found herself noting the changes his recent illness had wrought—the newly greying hair at his temples, the paler complexion, the not quite so robust appearance. Despite all of these, though, he was still an extremely intimidating figure of a man—as was his son—and Dale felt positively dwarfed by the pair of them as they eyed each other silently.

'Jack.' With a slight inclining of his head, Corey made the first acknowledgement.

'Corey.' His father's initial greeting was equally concise. 'I heard you were back. Although the drive out to the property was of too little significance for you to make, was it?'

Dale could see an ironic curve beginning to pull at Corey's mouth and she waited anxiously for him to set his father straight, but when it appeared he didn't intend to, she couldn't stop herself from interrupting.

'No, it wasn't!' she burst out hotly. 'As it so happens, he drove out to Tavener's Bridge the day he arrived in Karraparinka, but he wasn't allowed to see you.'

'Oh?' Ebony black eyes fixed her with a penetrating stare. 'Do I know you?'

'Keep out of this, Dale!' she was simultaneously ordered by Corey in a grating voice.

Defiantly ignoring the latter, she answered the former. 'I'm Dale Freeman, Mr Tavener, Lester and Irwin's niece. If you remember, I met you, rather briefly, on a couple of occasions before you were taken ill.'

'Hmm, I thought your face seemed familiar,' he

conceded shortly, his piercing gaze neither wavering, nor relenting. 'You're also the girl Kurt was seeing, and whom I now hear Corey is considering marrying, aren't you?'

Instinctively, Dale's own gaze darted to Corey. Was he planning to tell his father the truth or not? But someone else also saw her hesitation, causing another pair of eyes to turn in the same direction.

'Well, isn't she?' Jack Tavener demanded peremptorily of his son.

'If that's what you've heard, then I guess she must be,' came the rather—mockingly?—worded reply which had Dale suspecting the statement implied more than it actually revealed.

Apparently Corey's father must have thought so too, because he promptly fired back, 'And just what's that supposed to mean?'

'Exactly what you think it means!' retorted Corey no less sharply.

Momentarily, their glances locked unflinchingly, then a little to Dale's surprise, Jack Tavener yielded first. 'Well, *did* you drive out to the property?' he returned gruffly to his original subject.

With a direful, sidelong look at Dale, Corey nodded. 'But not in order to see me, obviously!'

Fearing another sardonic response—or worse, none at all—Dale recklessly launched herself into the fray once more. 'Naturally it was to see you, Mr Tavener,' she assured him earnestly. 'That's the reason Corey returned to Karra in the first place, and why he's waited around this long.'

From his expression it was difficult to tell whether the information had pleased Jack Tavener or not because of the frown it brought forth at her intervention.

'You seem to have a lot to say on the matter, don't you, young lady?' he commented somewhat dourly.

'Too much!' Corey's endorsement was caustically voiced. 'Go and read your magazines, Dale!'

'Why should I?' she half protested, half defied, her small pointed chin lifting challengingly.

'Because, once again, it has nothing to do with you!'

'Well now, if the two of you are going to get married ...' His father suddenly appeared to take the reverse approach, but whether just for the sake of opposing his son, Dale couldn't be certain.

'No, it's all right, Mr Tavener,' she demurred on a taut note, and trying desperately to disregard the gnawing pain in her chest that Corey's last remark had engendered. He couldn't have made it more clear that he neither needed nor wanted her—to defend him, or otherwise! 'But as this is the *public* bar,' she turned to Corey with a gibing glare, 'perhaps you'd feel more comfortable in the lounge. I shouldn't be able to hear a word from there!'

One corner of his attractively shaped mouth sloped tauntingly. 'Then it sounds most suitable!'

'Just consider it part of the service!' she quipped.

'You're too, too obliging!'

'Did someone say you two were planning to marry ... or divorce?' interposed Jack Tavener satirically.

Corey unexpectedly laughed, wryly. 'At least one's a distinct possibility,' he drawled, leaving his father to decide for himself just which it might be.

Since there never had been a proposal of marriage, Dale had no deduction to make, of course. Although that didn't prevent a pang of despair running through her at the thought of their inevitable parting, and she lowered her eyes swiftly in case they should traitorously provide a mirror for her unruly feelings.

When she looked up again it was to find herself alone, and with a disconsolate sigh she took a fresh packet of cigarettes from the dispenser on the wall behind her, broke it open and lit one. Whether Corey disapproved of her interest in his affairs or not, she was still apprehensive of the outcome of his meeting with his father, and as the minutes ticked away her nerves became unbearably stretched.

It was frustrating not knowing what was being said, and although she could make out the sound of their voices coming from the lounge, she couldn't distinguish any of the words, but she determinedly ignored the temptation to move closer to the door in order to hear more clearly. Not only was she not in the habit of eavesdropping, but as Corey had so bluntly informed her that it was none of her business, she was damned if she'd ever give him another opportunity to do so by displaying even the remotest interest—at least on the surface—in the matter again.

Occasionally, the muted rumble of Jack Tavener's voice would rise to a stentorian crescendo and have Dale unconsciously holding her breath in the expectation of seeing him go storming out of the building. Then, when he didn't appear, she would heave a sigh of relief and her agitation would subside to a less alarmed level once more. Apart from one instance, though—when it had suddenly snapped with the sting of a whip—she noted that Corey's tone remained remarkably even—an observation that momentarily had her experiencing a rueful kind of pity for his father. As she knew only too well from personal experience, it wasn't Corey's way to raise his voice in anger, but his method of using mocking irony to get his message across could be intolerably aggravating at times!

By the time an hour had passed, Dale had managed to puff her way nervously through four cigarettes—which was something of a record for her since she normally smoked only rarely; given directions—rather unnecessarily, she thought—concerning the whereabouts of the racetrack to one late visitor to the town; and flipped through every one of the new magazines without reading a single word.

The next thirty minutes were even worse, though, because now she didn't even have the magazines to at least partially occupy her mind, and when she finally saw Corey's father appear in the doorway she was both grateful and uneasy at the interruption.

'He's all yours,' he advised in a dry, but also somewhat uncompromising tone, so that it was impossible to deduce just what had eventuated during that long confrontation.

As a consequence, Dale's nerves weren't able to relax in the slightest and her voice was guarded as she queried, 'You're off to the races now, then, are you?'

'I'll see a few before I get Karl to drive me home,' he nodded.

'And—and Corey? Is he going out to the track with you too?' she asked constrainedly.

'No, he's packing,' was the flat reply which immediately set her pulse pounding with apprehension.

Packing, so he could go where? Tavener's Bridge . . . or Denham? Her pride wouldn't let her ask, nor would it allow her to evince any surprise at the information.

'I see.' She made a valiant effort to smile and sound as if that was precisely what she had been expecting to hear. 'Well, I hope you enjoy your afternoon at the races, Mr Tavener. I didn't get a chance to say so before, but I'm glad to see you're up and about again.'

'Thank you,' he acknowledged with a polite nod. 'And *I* hope our next meeting will be a more auspicious one.'

Dale gazed after his departing figure with a frown creasing her forehead. Had he meant the reason for, or the result of, their meeting had been inauspicious? she wondered. It took only a moment for her to decide just who was most likely to know the answer, and judging it improbable that anyone was going to require service in the bar during the next ten minutes, she headed determinedly down the hall.

CHAPTER NINE

APPROACHING Corey's room via the verandah, Dale drew a composing breath and knocked loudly on one of the opened french doors.

Inside, Corey laid a pair of jeans in the suitcase which rested on a luggage rack beside the wardrobe and then turned slowly to face her. 'Finished your reading, have you, angel?' he mocked, seeing her standing in the opening.

'No, I haven't, as a matter of fact,' she retorted, sauntering a few steps into the room. How could she have? She hadn't even started yet. 'It's just that your father told me you were leaving, so I thought I'd better come and see you.'

'In order to discover in which direction I'll be heading?' A dark brow quirked expressively.

Of course! Although she vowed she wouldn't enquire. She had been hoping to learn something from his expression, but unfortunately that was as unrevealing as his father's had been.

'Why should that matter to me?' she countered airily. 'It's none of my business where you go . . . as I'm sure you'll agree.'

Corey paced leisurely to within a metre or so of her, his amber gaze disturbing as it connected with an increasingly wary violet one. 'Then why did you come?'

'To—to find out exactly wh-when you're leaving, so I can make up y-your bill,' she fumbled, rather than flung at him as she would have preferred.

'In that case, I'll be making tracks this afternoon,' he told her impassively, but without—deliberately without! she surmised resentfully—giving an indication as to where he was going.

With a nod, she reluctantly began turning away, her brief flare of resentment submerging beneath a wave of despondency at the thought of him leaving so soon. If he was returning to Denham there was a distinct possibility she would never see him again. But now that she had the information she supposedly wanted, there was no real excuse for her to stay, and she blinked swiftly to ease the sudden burning sensation that attacked her downcast eyes.

'I—well—I wish you a safe journey,' she whispered throatily.

'With no recriminations for my disappearing . . . like last time?'

She recognised her own previous gibe, but more importantly, surely the implication was that he was returning to Denham! 'You didn't resolve your differences with your father?' she gasped in dismayed accents before she could stop herself from showing her concern.

'I thought you just said that didn't matter to you,' he reminded her tauntingly.

'It doesn't! Why should it?' she immediately retracted, shrugging defensively. 'You made it perfectly obvious my interest wasn't wanted!'

'Because that kind of interfering interest I could well have done without!'

'I was only trying to help!'

Corey's eyes swept sardonically over her slightly mutinous face. 'Except I don't happen to need you to fight my battles for me!'

'Well, you weren't going to tell your father you'd

been out to the property, or that he was the reason you'd returned to Karraparinka, were you?'

'Maybe because it didn't suit me to at that particular time.' His voice was abrasively cutting.

'So how was I to know that?' she glared at him huffily. 'Why didn't you say something beforehand?'

'I probably would have, if I'd known you intended taking over,' was the caustic retort which had her seething with indignation.

'I did not take over!' she protested vehemently. 'Although, if I had, perhaps it would have been no more than you deserved. After all, you had no compunction in taking over my life by telling everyone we were about to become engaged, did you?'

'For which you thanked me at the time, if I remember correctly,' drily.

'Well then, at least I showed some gratitude for your efforts on my behalf, didn't I?' she retaliated pungently.

'And you expected the same for yours?'

'I certainly wasn't anticipating condemnation, that's for sure!'

'So what did you figure on receiving? Something in this line, perhaps?' And, catching her unawares, he had pulled her to him and clamped his mouth arrogantly down on to hers before she could realise his intention.

Gasping, Dale dragged free of the devastating contact in a panic. 'No! You know damned well that never entered my head,' she panted jerkily.

'It did mine,' disclosed Corey almost wryly against the corner of her softly parted mouth seconds before inexorably taking possession of it again.

'Corey! Don't!' she pleaded desperately some thought-whirling moments later. He was decimating her defences, and the desire to respond was robbing her of what little control she did have left.

'Why? Because it's a waste of time with no one to see us?' His dusky-framed eyes fastened smoulderingly to hers.

'No, because I ...' Words failed her as her own deepening violet gaze clung helplessly to his. Loving him as she did, and knowing it could be the last time she ever saw him, made a combination that was impossible to deny, and when his lips sought hers yet again she finally surrendered to her innermost wishes, and with a partly sighed, partly sobbed, 'Oh, Corey!' she yielded willingly to the demands of his intoxicating touch.

Now, for the first time, Dale actively responded to his caresses. Entwining slender arms about his neck, her fingers threaded within his crisp hair, and she melted against his virile form unreservedly. Never before had she experienced such a rush of raw emotion and when, with a thickly voiced groan, Corey effortlessly swung her into his arms and carried her across to the bed, protest was the farthest thing from her mind. She loved him with every part of her being, and even if her actions did allow him to guess how irrevocably her feelings were involved, it just wasn't possible to conceal them any more.

Savouring the feel of his muscular length pressing against her, Dale recalled another time when she had shared Corey's bed with him, and had been as tantalisingly aware of his firm lips moving over the scented skin of her throat as she was now. Only on this occasion she wasn't anxious to escape, and she arched convulsively closer as a path of fire was trailed from the pulsing cord at the side of her neck to the hollow of her shoulder, and then the vulnerable base of her throat, before returning to her invitingly waiting mouth again.

With an uninhibitedness that was also new to her, she slid tentatively questing fingers beneath the silk knit of his shirt, her palms gliding slowly, wonderingly over the sinewed planes and ridges of his broad chest with its light covering of curling hair, and becoming conscious of a burgeoning sensation of pleasure on feeling his muscles bunch and grow at her exploring touch. He was as receptive to her caresses as she was to his!

Corey inhaled tautly, his breathing more uneven than Dale had ever known it as her hands proceeded to seek the smooth, solid flesh of his back, and his own hands beginning to trace the outline of her curving figure from flaring hip to shapely swelling breast with leisurely thoroughness. But when his hands deftly unfastened the shoulder buttons of her pink, square-necked top and she recalled that she hadn't worn a bra that morning in deference to the heat, it was Dale who drew in a trembling breath, although she made no move to impede the downward slide of the soft material. It wasn't that she was accustomed to such intimacies, but rather that where Corey was concerned she was helpless to control the warm wave of desire surging tumultuously through her body, and she thrilled to every touch of his knowing hands.

Almost as if in a dream she felt him cradle her naked breasts in those warm hands, and was startled by the strength of the emotions that overwhelmed her. It seemed as though she had only been half alive before, but now that she had discovered such ecstasy did exist she wanted it to continue for ever. She ached all over for him, and as his sensuous lips lowered to kiss and tease her nipples into aroused prominence, her hands clasped compulsively at the wide expanse of his shoulders, the ache inside her exploding into a torment of unparalleled wanting.

Then, with a despairingly incredulous shake of his head, Corey eased away from her slightly. 'Oh, God! I love you so much I can't keep my hands off you!' he groaned in a husky, impassioned tone.

Languorously purple eyes flickered bemusedly upwards. 'Wh-what did you say?' Dale queried shakily, disbelievingly. She couldn't possibly have heard him right, could she?

'I said, I love you,' he repeated in the same thick voice.

There was no doubting his sincerity—one look at the unbelievably tender expression on his face convinced her of that—but still she could only stare at him dazedly. 'Oh, Corey, I've wanted to hear those words so much, that now I don't know what to say,' she confessed tearfully, finally assimilating his avowal.

He brushed back her hair from a perspiration-dampened forehead with a gentle hand. 'Try a Yes in reply to the question . . . will you please marry me?' he suggested deeply.

'Oh, with all my heart, yes!' she complied immediately, fervently. And tangling her fingers in his midnight dark hair, she drew his head down to hers again to whisper devoutly against his lips, 'I love you, Corey Tavener! And I always will!'

The hair's breadth separating them was rapidly closed and with a sigh of contentment Dale wound her arms even more tightly about his neck, knowing she was loved in return. But when she was eventually released it was to find her thoughts dwelling on equally important matters.

'You know, you never did tell me whether you managed to settle your differences with your father or not,' she reminded him with a shy smile.

A teasing curve shaped his mouth lazily. 'But I thought you said . . .'

'Corey!' she cut in on him plaintively. 'Please! You know I didn't mean that.'

'I'm sorry,' he apologised ruefully. 'Yes, I've settled my differences with my father. Or at least I guess I have now.' His lips swept mirthlessly upward.

Dale looked at him somewhat askance. 'Meaning?'

He laughed engagingly. 'That after having decided to accept me back into the fold, as it were, he then promptly threatened to disown me again if, as he put it, I was fool enough *not* to marry you.'

'Oh!' His reply took her by surprise a little. She hadn't thought Jack Tavener had been particularly impressed with her because of her outspokenness. Then, with a grin starting to etch its way across her own lips, she eyed him with a mock-menacing glance. 'I see. So it was only to ensure you stayed in his good graces that you proposed to me, was it?'

'Uh-uh!' He shook his head decisively in veto. 'I as good as told you my intentions where you were concerned the afternoon I returned from Tavener's Bridge.' And in response to her frowned attempt at recollection, 'I said your association with Kurt wouldn't proceed any further if I had anything to do with it . . . remember?'

'But I thought you were just meaning . . .'

'Mmm, I know what you thought,' he grinned. 'You weren't entirely supposed not to.'

'But—but we'd only met the day before!' she exclaimed in a mixture of pleasure and amazement.

Corey bent to press a kiss to the corner of her softly parted mouth. 'I know what I like when I see it, angel, and Kurt or no Kurt, I intended to marry you as soon as I possibly could. And in that regard,' he suddenly began laughing again, 'I can't thank Opal enough for being such a malicious bitch. Through her efforts at slinging mud in your direction, she not only unwittingly provided me with the perfect opportunity to lay claim to you, but thereby she also gave me the means to eliminate Kurt's attentions to you.' He cupped her chin in a tender hand, his smile vanishing now just as quickly as it had appeared. 'I was scared stiff he might hurt you in some way.'

Her eyes misted uncontrollably at his concern. 'You mean, like he did Wanda?' she questioned softly.

He tensed sharply. 'You know about that?'

Dale nodded, catching at her lip with shining white teeth. 'I discovered it for myself at the races yesterday,' she explained slowly. 'I was watching Reuben playing with Peggy's children when he suddenly became annoyed over something, and it was for all the world as if I was looking at Kurt. The resemblance was unmistakable! Then Wanda herself came to see me after she'd been speaking to you this morning.' Her eyes flew to his anxiously. 'She apparently thought I was entitled to know the whole story since you and I were supposedly intending to marry.'

'*Are* intending to marry,' he corrected expressively, before sighing, 'I guess I should have know that's what she'd do. She's obviously been feeling a need to get it all out in the open for quite a while.' He half smiled crookedly. 'So now you finally know what happened, hmm?'

'Except for perhaps the most important piece of information of all,' she disagreed, and reached up to touch his lean cheek softly. 'Why didn't you ever deny it, Corey? That's what no one has been able to understand.'

'You still think that implies guilt of some kind?'

'No, of course not!' she protested, aghast. 'I know you're not the type to run out on your responsibilities, and—and I apologise for all those times when, through ignorance, I stupidly implied that you were.' She paused, sending him a humble glance from rueful eyes. 'I intended to tell you that yesterday, but unfortunately there just didn't seem to be a chance.'

Taking hold of the hand that still rested against his cheek, Corey proceeded to kiss each fingertip individually. 'Although there was a chance for another confrontation with Opal, by all accounts.' His eyes gleamed with amusement.

'Not by choice, I can assure you,' she returned on a wry note. 'But who told you about it?' She definitely hadn't mentioned it to anyone.

'Word gets around,' he drawled. 'I believe you also threatened to practise your judo on her.'

'Well, she wouldn't let go of my arm,' she defended, albeit none too straight-faced. 'Besides, I didn't feel very kindly disposed towards her, anyway. She kept acting as if she had some sort of prior claim or something on you.'

A look of surprise registered briefly on his face. 'I don't know why she should. I may have dated her at one time, but that was finished with years ago.'

'Opal apparently doesn't think so,' drily.

'Well, she'll know differently once we're married, won't she?' he grinned, lazily dismissive. 'But does this mean I can expect you to be practising the martial arts on me in future?'

'I doubt I'd be very successful if I did,' she laughed, eyeing his rugged length significantly. 'Although I may have been able to deal with Opal quite adequately, that would be about as far as my ability goes. You see, I tended to—er—overstate my experience somewhat, because actually I've never taken any lessons in judo at all. The only bits and pieces I know are those I picked up from a girl friend who took a short course in self-defence.'

An admission which drew a delighted laugh from Corey, but before he could speak she went on wryly, 'However . . . we seem to have digressed. Or would I be correct in assuming you're deliberately avoiding the question as to why you kept silent when you knew very well Wanda's pregnancy had absolutely nothing to do with you?' Her eyes sought his watchfully.

With a heavily expelled breath, Corey rubbed a hand distractedly around the back of his neck, his previous smiling expression altering to one that was both an ironic affirmation of her surmise and a ruefully resigned acknowledgement of her determination to know the answer. Rolling on to his back, he stared up at the ceiling, his hands clasped behind his head.

'I was asked—no, begged—not to deny it,' he finally revealed in a decidedly sardonic tone.

'By whom?' Dale gasped, propping herself up on one elbow in order to see him more clearly. 'Kurt?'

'And Louise.'

'But—but why did you agree?' She shook her head bewilderedly. 'I mean, why should they even *think* you would? You knew it was Kurt's child Wanda was expecting, didn't you?'

'Oh, yes, I knew all right,' he ground out roughly. 'He came whining to me first with the whole rotten story because he was too damned nervous to break it to his mother himself and wanted me to do it for him.'

'Did you?'

'Someone had to.'

'That still doesn't explain why you . . .'

'Took the blame?' he finished for her. A dry, self-mocking laugh issued from the column of his bronzed throat. 'Would you believe, to prevent Kurt from being thrown off the property by the old man?'

The irony of the situation wasn't lost on Dale either and she stared at him sympathetically. 'Because he wouldn't marry Wanda?'

'Because Wanda wasn't the first girl he'd put in the same predicament!' came the startling information. 'Only the previous one was considerate enough to leave town afterwards, but he was warned then that if it ever happened again he'd be out on his ear before he knew what had happened to him.'

'And that's why you were prevailed upon to make no denial,' she mused aloud, and only now beginning to realise just how lucky she had been in having her association with Kurt brought to an end. 'Although if Kurt was given a second chance, why weren't you too?'

Corey's lips slanted wryly. 'That's what everyone figured, but it seems more was expected of me.'

'Your father told you that today?' she deduced.

'More or less.'

'But once he'd given you that ultimatum, why didn't you say something then? If someone was going to be disowned, it should have been Kurt!'

'Hmm,' he pondered reflectively. 'Except that by

then I was so hellish annoyed by the fact that not once did he make any attempt to ask me if it was the truth—he just accepted it as such—and by his consequent reaction, that I'm afraid the excess of pride I told you about somehow managed to get in the way and I just flatly refused to tell him anything at all.'

'At which time I suppose he began to realise, to his dismay, that you did indeed intend to leave, but his pride wouldn't let him say anything either!' she reasoned caustically. Then, without giving him time to answer, she railed, 'Men! You'd cut off your noses to spite your faces—all in the name of pride!—and both you and your father should be ashamed of yourselves! I only wish I'd been here at the time. I wouldn't have let it come to that, I can tell you!'

Corey grinned incorrigibly, and in a sudden movement wrapped his arms around her, pinning her securely to his chest. 'I wish you'd been here too, angel,' he murmured lazily. 'Because then none of it would have happened. My bed would have been well and truly occupied by you long before Wanda thought of climbing into it.'

Dale flushed softly, prettily, the look in his eyes making it so difficult for her to think coherently that she willingly relinquished trying when his hand cupped the back of her head and slowly but surely urged her lips down to his.

Nevertheless, there were questions she still wanted to ask, although it was some considerable, but extremely satisfying, minutes later before her breathing had steadied enough to voice them.

'And—and was it pride that also made you stay away for so long?' she presumed with unusual throatiness.

'Of a sort, I guess,' he nodded whimsically. ' I didn't

intend for anyone—and least of all, the old man—to be in a position to accuse me of only returning for the sake of Tavener's Bridge.'

'So what *have* you been doing for the last eight years?' she asked of him interestedly.

'A bit of this and a bit of that,' he shrugged. 'Droving, buying and selling cattle—fortunately at the right times,' he laughed, 'managed a couple of properties, did a bit more wheeling and dealing, and finally succeeded in buying a place of my own.'

'At Denham,' she smiled.

'Uh-huh!'

'I asked Uncle Lester the other day just exactly where that was,' she confessed, dimpling.

His teeth shone startlingly white against his dark skin. 'And?'

'He said it was near what they call "Heartbreak Corner" and that the country there will either make you a fortune, or send you broke, and is quite capable of doing both in consecutive seasons,' she half grimaced, half laughed wryly. Her head tilted quizzically. 'Do you prefer it there to the Gulf?'

'Is that an indirect way of asking where we're going to live after we're married?' he countered in a teasing drawl.

Dale shook her head, smiling. 'It wasn't, but now that you've brought the matter up, I would be interested to know.'

'Do you have any preferences?'

'Only to be wherever you are,' she replied simply.

Corey's arms tightened about her stirringly. 'Then I guess it'll be the Gulf,' he advised in the deep, warm tone she loved so much. 'I was born here, my father was born here, and I think I'd like our children to be

born here too. There's something about this country
that gets into your blood . . . just like you do,' he smiled
at her captivatingly, 'and I still think of it as home.'

'Then here we'll stay,' Dale smiled back at him
readily. A moment later she waved a hand absently in
the direction of his unfinished packing. 'Is that where
you were heading for . . . Tavener's Bridge?'

'Uh-huh!' he affirmed laconically again.

With a frown beginning to form between her arched
brows, Dale eased herself into a sitting position, the
action reminding her selfconsciously of her state of
undress, and which despite Corey's bantering protest,
she proceeded to rectify.

'But won't it be a rather strained atmosphere out
there after—after all that's happened?' she queried
anxiously.

'Not without Louise and Kurt, I shouldn't think.'

'Without Louise and Kurt!' she echoed in disbelief.
'What do you mean without them? Just what did your
father tell you this morning, Corey?'

'Only that he and Louise had the grandfather of all
rows yesterday because of her efforts to prevent him
coming in to town, with the result that both she and
Kurt are, I believe, at the moment readying to leave
Tavener's Bridge for good,' he relayed with a total
unconcern Dale could well appreciate. 'It seems that
since all her plans for having Kurt and Karl inherit the
property have come to nought, she's decided she would
rather live elsewhere.'

'At your father's suggestion?'

'No, I understand it was all her own idea,' he
grinned. 'Although I gather he's rather relieved by the
decision. He apparently came to the conclusion some
time ago that he'd made a mistake in marrying her.'

Well, at least that was something! 'And Karl? He's leaving too, I suppose, is he?'

'As a matter of fact, he's not,' he surprised her by declaring. 'He's decided to stay. Do you think you'll be able to bear with the three of us?'

Dale slanted him a mock-menacing glance from beneath the cover of long, silky lashes. 'Are you and your father going to argue?'

'Possibly . . . probably,' he owned drily.

'I'm starting to think you both enjoy it, as Kurt once said he suspected,' she charged with rueful humour. 'But if you do have words I shall tell both of you off, you know that, don't you?' with a laugh.

'We'll take our chances,' he smiled broadly with her.

'You might be willing to, but will your father? I mean, he thought I had too much to say for myself this morning!'

'Not too much . . . just a lot,' corrected Corey drolly. 'Though you've no need to worry. Why do you think he said I'd be a fool if I didn't marry you? He prefers people to have something to say for themselves, and especially,' reaching up to twist one of her curls about his finger, 'when it's a slip of a girl who reminds him of his first wife.'

'I do?' she quizzed in amazement.

'You do,' he confirmed indolently. 'You have that same air of being able to wrap your menfolk around your little finger.'

'Is that what your mother used to do to him?' she chuckled delightedly.

'Did she ever!'

'And now he thinks I'll be able to do the same with you?'

Corey's expression was the driest she had ever seen. 'He's counting on it.'

'Well, well,' she grinned teasingly as she lightly traced an imaginary pattern across his chest with the tip of her forefinger. 'That does sound promising, doesn't it?'

Faster than she would have believed possible, Dale abruptly found herself swung on to her back with Corey leaning over her. 'You little witch!' he smiled down at her lovingly. 'You know damned well you'll have all three of us eating out of your hand before you've been there a month. You've already got me to the stage where I can't think of anything but you!'

'Have I really, Corey?' she asked diffidently, resting her hands on his shoulders. She still felt like pinching herself to make certain it wasn't all a dream.

He bent to kiss her lingeringly, reassuringly. 'You have, angel,' he vouched deeply. 'I love you so much I hate letting you out of my sight.'

'Oh, Corey!' she breathed adoringly. 'I never knew I could feel about anyone the way I do about you. I'm so happy I feel like crying. Right from that first morning when you walked into the hotel, almost my every thought seems to have revolved around you.' Her eyes started to shine with a twinkling light. 'Much to Kurt's annoyance on occasion, I might add!'

'Such as that night he stormed out of the bar?' he drawled idly.

'Mmm, even before he refused to join the search party he hadn't been too pleased with all my questions regarding your visit to the property. But talking about the bar . . .!' Her expression suddenly changed from enraptured contentment to wide-eyed alarm. 'Oh, good lord, I only meant to be away for a few minutes!

Anyone could just walk in and help themself!'

'On the main day of the races?' Corey cast her an expressive glance. 'We're probably the only two left in town!'

Since the hotel's business had been exactly nil so far that morning, she didn't doubt he was right, and she relaxed complacently within the circle of his arms again. 'Yes—well, in any case, I don't suppose a few more minutes will make much difference, will they?' Her eyes sought his enticingly.

'Now that, my love, just depends on how you're planning to occupy them,' Corey murmured huskily against her already parting lips.

Harlequin Plus

A WORD ABOUT THE AUTHOR

Although for many years she has considered herself an Australian, Kerry Allyne was in fact born in England. Her early childhood was uneventful, she remembers, until her father came home one day and began talking about emigrating to Australia. When they eventually arrived in Australia Kerry took to her new land with a passion.

During the family's first years "down under," she explored as much of the country as she could, journeying northward into Queensland and out onto the Great Barrier Reef, and sometimes south through New South Wales into Victoria. "Always there was something new to see and experience."

These youthful travels were to be tucked away until the time came when Kerry began writing in earnest. But first she returned to England for a working holiday. Then, back in Australia, she met her husband-to-be, an engineer.

After marriage and the birth of two children, the family headed north to Summerland, a popular surfing resort, where today they run a small cattle farm and an electrical-contracting business.

When her youngest child started school, Kerry Allyne decided to fill her days by writing a novel. Her attempt was entitled *Summer Rainfall* and was published in 1976 as Romance #2019. "Following the doubts that accompanied its mailing," she says, "the thrill of having it accepted was totally unbelievable!"

Kerry Allyne says that rural Australia is a great source of inspiration for a writer—"one that gives me great enjoyment to try to capture on paper."

Readers of Kerry's Romances will agree that she has succeeded admirably in this task!

Legacy of
PASSION
BY CATHERINE KAY

A love story
begun long ago
comes full circle…

Venice, 1819: Contessa Allegra di Rienzi, young, innocent, unhappily married. She gave her love to Lord Byron—scandalous, irresistible English poet. Their brief, tempestuous affair left her with a shattered heart, a few poignant mementos—and a daughter he never knew about.

Boston, today: Allegra Brent, modern, independent, restless. She learned the secret of her great-great-great-grandmother and journeyed to Venice to find the di Rienzi heirs. There she met the handsome, cynical, blood-stirring Conte Renaldo di Rienzi, and like her ancestor before her, recklessly, hopelessly lost her heart.

Choose from this great selection of early Harlequins—books that let you escape to the wonderful world of romance!*

*Some of these book were originally published under different titles.